The Infinite
Worlds of Maybe
by Lester Del Rey

For every situation there are two realms of possibility: Columbus did/did not discover America; the North/South won the Civil War. That is the intriguing premise of this highly unusual adventure by one of the most distinguished authors of science fiction.

When Bill Franklin's father disappears suddenly, Bill faces the challenge of seeking out this fascinating world of duality. Mr. Franklin, a scientist, has apparently set off to prove his theory that the "infinite worlds of maybe" do indeed exist; he leaves behind only some jumbled notes, a box-like machine, and spacesuits. From these, Bill and his physics professor eventually are able to project themselves into a series of astonishing new worlds where they are confronted by terrifying dangers. The end to this fascinating search comes with the revelation of an important discovery that is to have lasting implications in all of their lives.

Lester Del Rey's strongly written adventure will appeal to all who enjoy fine science fiction.

The Infinite Worlds of Maybe

The Infinite Worlds of Maybe

by Lester Del Rey

Holt, Rinehart and Winston

NEW YORK, CHICAGO, SAN FRANCISCO

Contents

The Infinite Worlds of Maybe

A Frightening Letter

BILL FRANKLIN'S HAND SHOOK. HE stared at it. And his mind, trying to recover from the shock it had just received, began forming odd thoughts:

It's nothing but a piece of white paper. Dad put it into a typewriter and made some marks on it called letters. These letters formed into things called words. And these harmless little words strung together in things called sentences are making my hand shake. That's very funny—very strange.

Except that it was not at all funny; nor was it strange. Define it as he would, the thing he held in his hand was still a letter, and it had knocked the props out from under his world. He needed advice—counsel and comfort—but irony lay in the fact that the only person he could go to was the one who had written the letter and put himself beyond reach.

There was no place to turn.

Then, quite sternly, he banished that nonsense from his mind. There were plenty of intelligent, sympathetic people on the campus who would be glad to listen.

Reaction from the sudden shock touched him. It brought a sound from his throat. Almost a chuckle. And a wry, inner voice whispered: *Name three.* With somewhat solider control, now, he answered the whisper. *Ridiculous!* He was no longer a child. He was Bill Franklin—nineteen, going on twenty. Nor was he alone on a desert island. As an undergraduate at Queens College, he was acquainted with dozens of people.

The name of one of these popped instantly into his mind. Neal Adams, scientist, Professor of Applied Physics at Queens.

I wonder why I thought of him? Bill asked himself the question as he folded the note, slipped it into his shirt pocket, and began wandering aimlessly through the big house—the house that had recently been turned gloomy and empty by the death of his mother —a house in which the light had gone out.

As was his nature, he kept his mind resolutely off of the old warmth and cheer and the wonderful love and closeness of the three of them there in the big house—turned his mind from thoughts of that kind because he refused to feel sorry for himself. There was no point in self-pity.

After a while, he left the house and went to his father's back-yard laboratory. It was a converted carriage house and was as much a machine shop as a laboratory because most of his father's strange inventions were of a heavy nature.

It had been here that Sam Franklin, the man many called "that crackpot inventor," had created the almost indestructible foam-rubber automobile tire that made him independently wealthy.

Now the laboratory was as lonely and gloomy as the house Bill had just left.

He idled about the laboratory for a few more minutes. But then, after making his decision, he hesitated no longer, getting into his car and heading directly for Faculty Row.

He found Professor Adams on his front porch, a pipe in his mouth and an examination paper in his hand. Looking up pleasantly, the professor said, "Hello, Bill. Glad you dropped in. I was hoping for an excuse to knock off on these papers."

Neal Adams looked young for the post he held. Not over forty and possibly younger. But there was something in his manner, in his quiet gray eyes, that instilled confidence.

"I need your advice," Bill said. "I found a letter when I got home from my last class, and—well, I don't know what to do."

"I'll be happy to give you whatever advice I can," Neal Adams said as he tapped his pipe out into the ashtray beside him. As Bill dropped down onto the top porch and sat silent, Adams regarded him keenly for a few moments before he asked, "Just what is the problem, Bill?"

"I—I don't quite know how to put it. You know that since Mother died, Dad has probably been in worse shape than he appeared to be." Bill stopped suddenly, fumbling. "No—there's no reason you should be aware of that."

"On the contrary. I talked to your father several times since the funeral. He is a strong man, no doubt of that—a lot of quiet strength. But I saw the change."

"Dad liked you," Bill said.

"And I like him, but why are you putting that *liked* into the past tense?"

"Because he's gone."

"Gone? I don't understand."

"I guess we might as well get straight to it. This is the letter I found when I got home. And Dad was gone."

He handed Neal the missive that had made his hand shake and then stared at the bottom step. After a few moments, he looked up quickly.

"Will you read it aloud, Professor? I want to hear

it from someone else. I want to see if it said what I think it did or whether I'm dreaming."

This outburst brought a moment's study from Adams. Then he turned his eyes back to the letter. "Of course," he said quietly. Then he began reading.

"Dear Bill:

"You and I have always been frank and open with each other. We've never beat around the bush, so I'll make this direct and to the point.

"I am leaving this plane on which we live to seek worlds that may not even exist."

That last statement pulled Adams up abruptly. His pause was long enough to be significant, but when he went on it was in the same quiet voice.

"You may think that I have gone out of my mind, and perhaps by some standards, I have. But I must go forward, along paths which, by my own standards, seem logical.

"Do not, my son, as a result of this letter, run to the police and institute a search for a missing father. The places I will go, if I am successful, will not be in realms to which the police have access.

"As you know, since I invented the tire that made us financially independent, my research has branched into what might be called less practical fields—but I believe fields just as solidly scientific. You and I have discussed my theory of the existence of other worlds —worlds of infinite possibility. And once the theory is accepted, these become worlds of infinite probability. You will recall that we spoke of them as worlds of maybe.

"In order to hold this letter to a minimum, I'll state quite simply that I think I've found a way to enter these other planes of existence.

"And now for the really important part of this letter, my son—an attempt to make you understand the abruptness of my decision and why I leave you behind. Since the death of your mother, Bill, things have changed for me. The light that guided me has gone out. The threads that held me to this world into which you were born have been broken. I do not seek to be flowery or poetic—my only desire is to shape a concept you will grasp, and to make the sting of my deserting you less sharp."

Professor Adams stopped and made a leisurely gesture out of picking up his pipe and tamping tobacco into it. But he picked up the letter and went on without lighting the pipe.

"Leaving you alone brought a great sense of guilt, and I overcame it only when I ceased to regard you as a boy and saw you as a man. And you are close to being a man, Bill—closer than you realize. Your financial security—the things for your welfare—have been arranged, and the risks of this venture must be mine and mine alone. That is what I beg you to understand, my son—that the injustice of subjecting you to the possible peril of this journey I must make is far greater than leaving you to build a life in your own familiar world. Thus, I seek to prove my love by doing the difficult thing. Believe me—taking my

son with me on this great adventure was a temptation
to which I almost surrendered.

"But I shall not drag this letter on. The writing
of it has been the most difficult job I ever undertook.

"Goodbye, my son. Have faith. Tell yourself as you
grow into strong, productive manhood that I am still
in existence in some other world whole and happy
and fulfilling my destiny.

"All my love,
"Dad."

There was silence. Somewhere in the grass a cricket
made a cheerful comment. Professor Adams folded the
letter and handed it back.

Bill was not sure what sort of a reaction he'd
expected. But he discovered that he had unconsciously
braced himself against it. Ridicule at the wild idea set
forth in the letter? Hardly. Neal Adams was not that
kind of man. Unbelief? That was not too difficult to
imagine. Would Professor Adams offer a superficial
sympathy and suggest that Bill go to the police? Or
would he bow out gracefully, not wishing to become
involved with crackpots?

Adams launched himself into none of these directions. He did not react at all. To all outward ap-
pearances, he could have just finished with another
class report. But Bill assumed the worst, thinking, He
doesn't intend to help me. He's looking for words to
back out gracefully.

Adams made a long ceremony out of lighting his

pipe. Bill conquered an urge to jump up and run. Then Adams spoke.

"You're ashamed of your father, aren't you, Bill?"

"Ashamed of him! Why I—I am not!"

The urge to cut and run came even stronger, but a new aspect held him. Neal Adams was not quite as Bill had previously classified him. There was more power in the man; a keener perception; a far greater depth. With a single sharp question, he'd uncovered a vein of guilt in Bill.

"I think," Neal Adams went on, "that we should talk about you at this point, not your father."

Quick hostility clawed at Bill, choking off his rejoinder. Adams was clearly aware of this, but he observed it quietly.

"I think perhaps you came here to get a pat on the head and a bucketful of sympathy."

"But you said I'm ashamed."

"That *was* quite abrupt—and somewhat brutal. But if I were less than frank, I would be doing you and your father no service whatever. I think, Bill, this is a time for frankness. I admired your father. Therefore, naturally, I have not been unaware of his son. And I've arrived at some conclusions about you. In the first place, you communicate badly."

Bill was completely at sea. No one had ever talked to him in this manner before. "Well, I—"

"That is another way of saying that you're a loner. You have very few friends around the campus. Am I right?"

"Well, I'm always pretty busy—"

"That is a result rather than a cause. You *become* busy at other things in order to fill the time left empty by your withdrawal."

Bill was stunned. Neal Adams, out of a clear sky, had slashed ruthlessly to the heart of what Bill considered to be his own secret.

He'd long been aware of his shortcoming—his inability to mix, to open himself to friends, to become a part of campus life. But this was not his fault. He had analyzed the problem and learned to live with it.

"It's just the way some people are," he explained.

"Oh?" Neal Adams exhibited quick interest. "Tell me."

"Well, it's a matter of inherent personality. Some people are naturally social. Some aren't. I'm one who isn't—who can't open up to people."

"I see," Adams replied, as though that explained everything. "Then you enjoy staying off by yourself."

"Of course not."

Bill floundered miserably. He resented Neal Adams' harsh intrusion into his personal life. He hadn't come to be psychoanalyzed. He was there to talk about Dad's letter and he thought Neal Adams was being unfair.

And Adams no doubt sensed this. He said, "All right, let's talk about your father."

"He was a great scientist!" Bill countered belligerently.

"Certainly. And you would fight anyone who denied it. But you're basically a peaceful person, so you've withdrawn in order to avoid the possible need to fight."

"I don't get your point!" Bill cried desperately. "I don't know why you're talking this way!"

Neal Adams leaned forward. "Easy, Bill—easy. I know what you're going through. It's tough, and I want to help. But sometimes help takes cruel forms. When a man is faced with a crisis, he needs every weapon he can get. And facing the truth about ourselves is often a powerful weapon, the difference between victory and defeat. That is why I'm asking you to listen to me."

There was a pause. "All right," Bill said finally. "I'll listen."

"Good. Now to begin with, your father's scientific greatness took some startling forms as evidenced by this letter."

"Then you don't see it as a wild—"

"Definitely not, but one thing at a time. Let's stick with you. You've retired into yourself because, while you believe in your father completely, others might be prone to ridicule and jeer. Great scientists, men ahead of their times, had always been ridiculed and jeered at by the unthinking."

"Then you're calling me a coward," Bill said bitterly.

"No such thing. You've been defending your father in the only way you knew, the way you've grown up with. And that isn't cowardice, it's bravery."

"You're very kind." There was acid in Bill's tone, but Adams ignored it.

"Your father was not entirely blameless. Totally preoccupied with his work, there was much he overlooked."

"It wasn't his fault. Dad *was* a great scientist. His mind had to be on his work. Where else could it be? When Mom was here, when the three of us were together, it was wonderful. We didn't need anyone else."

"No doubt," Neal Adams said gently. "But now your mother and father are gone. And you do need someone."

At this point, Bill sensed a crisis within a crisis— one that had shaped and had to be faced right there on that porch. He had to accept or reject Neal Adams and this constituted a fork in his road.

The decision was understandably difficult. It was as though Neal Adams had ripped off some of his skin and the ripping had been painful.

But, along with the anger and humiliation, there was something else—something that surprised Bill.

A sense of relief. A strange feeling of new freedom. Something almost magical when he thought about it. The dread and despair he'd brought with him was at least partially dissolved; replaced by a feeling of excitement and anticipation. And he heard his own halting words.

"I appreciate your interest and if . . . if we could sort of . . . work together on this thing . . ."

Neal Adams did not make a production out of it. He scratched a match and let it burn as he said, "I was hoping you'd ask me."

"Then you *will*."

He shook the match out with a quick gesture that signified agreement. "All the way. Now first off, let's make sure we understand each other. I assume that neither of us see your father as having slipped his trolley. We both regard this letter as a mark of some scientific progress he made."

"It refers to something he's been working on for a long time. A theory and a machine."

"The letter and some references he made during our conversations give me a sketchy idea. But there's one thing you're forgetting. The time of night," Adams smiled. "Let's knock it off and hit the sack. Tomorrow's another day, as some brilliant joker once said."

Bill laughed and it occurred to him that he'd never felt so free and easy with anyone.

"How would you like to use my spare bedroom tonight?"

"Thanks," Bill said, "but I think I'd rather go home. I feel a little different about things now, and—"

"I understand. We'll get together tomorrow. By fortunate circumstance, it's Saturday. Call me when you wake up."

Bill's warm feeling as he drove home was like a overcoat.

A wonderful feeling.

He had a friend!

Battle Scene

"I THINK YOUR FATHER expected you to follow him," Neal Adams said. "Or at least, try to."

This startled Bill. "In that case, wouldn't he have taken me with him?"

"It's only a hunch."

"Maybe he meant that he'd come back some day."

"Possibly, but he made no reference to it." Neal Adams' eyes roamed thoughtfully over the mass of complicated machinery there in Sam Franklin's laboratory. "As I said, it's just a hunch. But this—I never saw such a mass of complication in my life. It makes a person feel totally inadequate."

Bill said, "Dad could carry more complex detail in his mind than ten average men. That was why much that he said sounded—well, zany. When he spoke of something it was from a basis of background material he was entirely familiar with. It just didn't occur to him that the people he talked to didn't have the foggiest notion of what lay behind his statements."

Neal Adams had picked up a notebook from one of the benches and was thumbing through it. He smiled wryly. "This data bears you out. It's highly technical, of course, but to put it in a simplified comparison, I'd say it's like a literary thesis with every second word missing."

"That was Dad. I think he figured whoever read the thesis should know the missing words without having to be told."

As Neal Adams surveyed the laboratory, a look of frustration, of anger, touched his face. "What fools we are!" he muttered. "What unthinking fools!"

Bill was startled. But he said nothing. He waited and Adams went on.

"The fantastic work your father was doing here and the opportunity I had to participate! But no! I was always so busy with more *important* things."

"I see what you mean. But you're being too hard on yourself. Dad liked to work alone."

Adams brushed that aside impatiently. "That wasn't

true. He was willing, often eager, to talk of what he was doing."

"Then I'm more at fault than you. I was his son. I was right here all the time."

"Well," Adams said grimly, "none of that negates the fact that we've got a job to do here. A big job." He turned his eyes quickly upon Bill. "Do you feel up to it?"

The question was a direct challenge, and Bill knew it. The feeling of warmth came again, although Adams was not smiling. On the contrary, his tone was crisp. In essence, he was saying, If you want to drop out, now is the time. We are separating the men from the boys. If necessary, I'll go on by myself.

"You bet I feel up to it!"

"It will be dangerous."

"That didn't stop Dad."

"Fine."

Bill wanted to shout and run around the laboratory from sheer exuberance. A friend! Someone close to work with, to share with. It had been so difficult before. Now it was so easy.

"Do you really think Dad expected me to follow him?"

"I think he hoped that you would be able to. Now tell me—exactly how much do you know about all this?"

"Very little."

"Then we'll pool the little I know with yours and go on from there." The grimness was gone from

Adams' manner—replaced with perhaps a touch of the excitement Bill felt. "There is an old saying that machines are made by geniuses for fools to run. Let's assume that's true and go to work."

"I'm ready."

"Then, to begin with, what do you know about the power source in this laboratory?"

"It comes in over there—a special cable. Light and heat come in off the town circuits. Nothing special about that. But Dad had a special, high-capacity cable installed."

"Is there a main switch?"

"Over here."

"Then you'd better break the circuit before we electrocute ourselves."

Bill went to a big gray box and opened it. There was a blue flash as he opened the switch.

"That's better," Adams said. "Now we can do a little investigating. Let's start with this." He indicated a clumsy-looking garment lying on a nearby table. It was plugged into an electric cord that was, in turn, attached to a complicated set of boxes. "It looks like a diving suit, but I doubt if it is."

"Wired for heat, maybe."

"Or something else." Adams touched a black knob. "This appears to be a switch." He turned it.

Immediately, a faint humming sound was audible. They looked at each other in surprise, listening.

"What do you think it is?" Bill asked.

"A power signal of some sort. It couldn't be anything else. Are you sure you cut off the power source?"

"I'm positive."

"Then this suit must be connected to the lighting system."

Bill shook his head. "I'm sure it isn't. That's one thing I know. Dad never connected anything to the town system. He was afraid of blowing out all the lights."

The sound was increasing steadily in volume. Neal Adams' fingers remained poised on the knob, but he did not switch it off. "Then the power can only come from storage—batteries—and it could hardly be dangerous."

They waited. The sound increased in timbre and volume. It became deeper—an awesome sound, indicating, beyond all doubt, a vast flow of tremendous power.

Adams snapped off the switch.

"We don't have to be very smart to figure that one out," he said. "There is an incredible power supply in here somewhere."

"And that suit took it," Bill marveled. "If I'm any judge at all, the power we heard would have blown every fuse in town if it was turned loose without resistors and transformers. But that suit took it."

"Let's find the power source first—the batteries."

"Batteries big enough to store power like that? The laboratory wouldn't hold them."

"We must start accepting miracles," Adams said, "or at least contradictions of laws we know about."

Bill was still bemused. "You're right. That was the scariest sound I ever heard in my life." Then Bill's eyes brightened as he laid a hand on Adams' arm. "Suppose I try it out! I could put on that suit and . . ."

There was no answering enthusiasm. "I don't think we'll start dressing for the occasion until we know more about the costumes. There's at least a week's work here, just sorting things out so that our finite minds can begin to grasp their significance."

"Then let's get started!"

"Not so fast. It would be far wiser to make haste by going slowly."

"Then how *do* we start?"

"I think some briefing is in order. Suppose we sit down quietly somewhere and you can tell me all you know about your father's theory."

Bill turned his eyes quickly away. "I'll try, of course. But I'm not very good at communicating. Bringing things out . . ."

"Just do your best. You may be surprised. Let's go out on your back-yard swing where it's cooler."

For a few moments, Bill found Adams' restraint frustrating. He wanted to plunge in headfirst and dig out the many answers that lay about them. But then the wisdom of Adams' discipline asserted itself and Bill found satisfaction in controlling his enthusiasm.

"I'll do my best," he said.

Adams stopped at the swing and Bill went on into the house and brought back a couple of glasses and a family-sized Coke from the refrigerator. "About all I can do," he said, "is try to relay it to you the way Dad gave it to me. But it was kind of hit-and-miss. It didn't make much sense to me."

"We'll apply two minds to it and see what happens."

"He started with a question. He said, suppose Columbus had gotten cold feet during his voyage and turned back before he sighted land. Then he asked me what sort of world I thought we'd have as a result. All I could tell him was a different world."

Adams sipped his Coke and waited.

"Then," Bill went on, "he said he was sure that world existed."

Adams pursed his lips thoughtfully. "He certainly opened an area for vast conjecture."

"He called them worlds of possibility. He said there were many places in history where a tiny change would have given us a different world. Some could depend on things so delicate that the Heisenberg Uncertainty Principle might make them pure chance. For instance, the mutation of some virus in the past that might have rendered it fatal to, say, dinosaurs and given mammals quicker control of the earth."

Adams' eyes were narrowed in concentration. "Suppose, instead of Columbus' getting here first, the Chinese had crossed the Pacific in 900 and settled the Pacific Coast. They would certainly have disputed the terrain with the Spaniards coming up from the south and would no doubt have been far stouter antagonists than the superstition-ridden Aztecs."

"Dad thought that for every such decision at least

two worlds exist, one stemming from each of the possibilities. He said that of course this plurality of worlds seems to violate the law of mass energy conservation, but for that matter so does the coming into existence of even one world."

"So far as laws are concerned," Adams said, "I'm sure we could find some that even the existence of life itself violates—if life were not here to prove otherwise."

"You've got a point," Bill admitted.

"Worlds of infinite possibility," Adams murmured as though hypnotized by the idea. "I'm afraid I'm not quite the calm theoretician I thought I was. I'd like to get back to that laboratory. Suppose we have another go at it?"

Bill was certainly more than willing. They hurried back. Surrounded again by the maze of complex construction, Adams muttered ruefully, "Well, no scientific gremlins have straightened things out in our absence."

Bill's eagerness had returned. "Let's turn that suit on again. We didn't get killed the last time."

Adams smiled briefly, acknowledging an understanding of Bill's enthusiasm, but at the same time resisting it. "There are three more suits stacked there in the corner. Do you suppose they represent various stages of experimentation?"

"Could be. I remember that Dad used to sit crosslegged with the suits around him like a tailor making clothes."

"This," Adams said, picking up a tubelike mechanism, "looks like a periscope. But it doesn't seem to have an eyepiece."

"It could be a receiving tube of some kind."

"But I don't find any place to attach it to the suit."

"It probably plugs into this cabinet somewhere. The cabinet is very important. Dad used to work at it for days on end."

"Perhaps it holds the power supply."

"We can look for batteries inside."

The search was negative. There were three removable plates in the cabinet, but they found nothing inside but a complicated maze of wiring. After fifteen minutes of research, Adams straightened and rubbed his back.

"It has to be a control unit. It may step power up or reduce it, but it's definitely not a source."

"Then where?" Bill began blankly.

"We've got to decipher the notes," Adams said.

Bill grinned. The excitement of the investigation and the easiness of the rapport he and Adams had achieved, gave him a freedom of his own.

"Maybe not."

Adams' frown questioned.

"You said it yourself," Bill reminded. "Machines are built by geniuses for fools to operate."

"It's true. Nevertheless . . ."

The grin deepened. "The man who buys a car doesn't have to take a course in engineering before he drives it."

Adams allowed his frown to remain. It hid his true reaction—pleasure at the manner in which Bill was breaking through his shell of restraint.

"We won't argue the point," Adams said with the faintest of smiles. "But we'll study the notes all the same."

"If you say so," Bill replied cheerfully. He was back at the suit. "This is made of some kind of plastic. I think Dad invented the material himself."

"I wouldn't doubt it. I'm beginning to think he also invented the laws he needed to make his idea practical."

Bill stopped suddenly. His eyes took on an added glow as he stared at the suit. "Why—why he was— *great*." It was as though a great truth had suddenly dawned on him.

Adams was not unaware of the dawning. Nor did he consider it mawkish or overly sentimental. "At the risk of boring you with sayings, A prophet is without honor . . ."

"I'm beginning to realize that." Becoming self-conscious, Bill snatched quickly at the suit. "There's a place here in the shoulder to plug something in."

The moment was over.

"The batteries, perhaps," Adams said, "if we can ever find them."

Bill indicated a heavy outlet on the wall behind one of the workbenches. "Maybe there. For testing?"

"Could be. But for testing only. Your father obviously used this equipment to go into other worlds.

And he certainly couldn't have made it while attached to the wall of this shop by an electric cord. He had to take his power with him."

"Well, there certainly aren't any batteries in sight, except those on the bench there, those flashlight batteries."

Adams had paid no attention to them. Now he picked one up.

"Plain zinc jacket. No markings. Let's test them." There were several flashlights lying around the laboratory, some battered up pretty badly. Adams took the one most apparently functional, unscrewed its cap, and slipped the batteries in. He screwed the cap back on and snapped the switch. Nothing happened but an instant blackening of the bulb behind the reflector.

"Burned it out." He glanced at Bill and then about the shop. "I'm beginning to get a hunch. Do you see a pair of rubber gloves around anywhere?"

"Over there." Bill retrieved the heavy gloves and Neal Adams slipped them on.

"Do any of those flashlights work?" Adams asked.

Bill found one that did.

"Bring it over here and hold it for me."

Adams went to the place where the lighting conduit entered the shop.

While Bill watched, Adams opened the incoming wire and exposed the two ends. He put the two batteries in concentric position and touched them to the circuit.

Every light in the place blew instantly.

"Incredible!" Adams marveled as they stood in darkness relieved only by a feeble flashlight beam. "Two one-inch flashlight batteries blew the whole place out. I think, if we wanted to, we could blow out every light in town—including the street lamps—with just these two little batteries."

"How could it be possible?"

While Bill used a flashlight to find some fuses and replace the blown ones, Adams replied "I'd say the *why* is more important than the how, right now. Your father certainly devised a way to concentrate tremendous power into a very small storage area. I'm wondering why it was necessary."

"The transition from one of his worlds to another must require it."

"Exactly," Adams agreed. "And now, shall we take the next step?"

"The next step? Sure. What is it?"

"Suppose we apply the power in these two small batteries to this periscope mechanism? What do you think might happen?"

"All we could do would be to blow it out."

"I doubt it. Remember that power hum."

"But how do we make the connection?" Bill asked.

"There's a small drawer just here—at the base. It would hold the two batteries nicely."

"That's true, but I don't see any contact points."

"They may be inside. If we put the batteries . . . like so . . . perhaps that makes contact when we close the drawer."

Perhaps they did—perhaps they didn't. At any rate, when Adams closed the drawer, nothing happened.

"Maybe it's just a small storage bin," Bill said.

"That could be, but then too, there may be a switch someplace. It's hardly likely that a man with your father's skill and thoroughness would use the opening and closing of a drawer as his control element."

Bill said nothing but he was annoyed with himself. He appreciated Neal Adams' tactful method of ignoring his stupidity, but that didn't change the fact that it *was* stupidity. He wished his college training had been along lines other than languages and liberal arts. Mechanical engineering and electronics would stand him in better stead at the moment.

"What's this?" he asked.

"The switch, I'm sure. I think you've found it."

Bill had pointed to what appeared to be a switch but he wished Neal Adams hadn't made his reply sound so much like a compliment. A little more of that sort of thing and he would start feeling like a backward child. You didn't need a course in engineering to find a simple switch even though it was rather cleverly hidden.

"Shall I push it?"

"Go ahead," Adams replied. "We may be on the threshold of . . . something. But only heaven knows what."

The muted snap of the switch—and they waited tensely for results. The next thirty seconds was like an hour. Then a faint hum was heard. This grew louder and then faded. Then Bill's eyes went to the other mechanical unit—the one upon which Neal Adams' attention was already riveted. It looked somewhat like the end of an unmounted video tube and had been previously referred to by Neal Adams as possibly being a component of the periscope complex.

Now it was activating. It became a brightly lit white screen. Then a sudden black and white image faded in.

It was a battle scene. Uniformed troops were fighting in the streets of a modern city. As they watched, a helmeted figure moved out from behind a ruined wall and hurled a grenade at an advancing squad. The invading group deployed instantly, flinging themselves toward shelter.

The grenade exploded and the squad emerged and again moved forward—all except three who were killed by the grenade.

Moving grimly and efficiently in commando style, they zeroed in on the wall from behind which the grenade thrower had emerged. Assaulting the barricade from three angles, they poured in lethal fire, their short-barreled rifles jerking with each shot. A moment later the single defender of the position came erect and fell dead across the wall.

The squad moved on, seasoned fighting men evidently engaged in a mop-up operation.

As he stared at the screen, Bill caught a movement of Neal Adams' hand. Adams had found a likely looking knob. He turned it and a new scene faded in. It was a long shot of a city partially in ruins, the same city, no doubt, in which the commando action had just taken place.

Then without warning, the screen flashed white and went dead.

They stared at the blank tube, the dead silence screaming around them—stared for quite a while before Bill lifted his eyes and met those of Neal Adams. Bill was tense with excitement, but he took his cue from the quiet, thoughtful reaction of his physicist friend. "What do you think it was?" he asked.

"I don't know. A scrap of newsreel film? A few panels from the late movie?"

"You mean it's a hoax of some sort?"

Bill's reaction was one of anger. He felt this was a reflection on his father's integrity. But Adams sensed this and reassured him.

"We don't know what your father meant this machine to be. It could be an ordinary television set." The shake of Bill's head was positive. "He wouldn't waste his time on ordinary things."

"I'm sure he wouldn't. Let's close up shop and talk about it outside. It's hot in here."

Bill's thoughts were a chaotic jumble as he nodded and started toward the door. But when Adams didn't follow, he turned.

"Just one little thing, first," Adams said.

Bill watched as Adams unscrewed the cap on one of the flashlights and took out the batteries. He retrieved the unmarked pair from the drawer in the periscope and inserted them in the flashlight. He screwed the cap back on and nothing happened. After staring thoughtfully at the flashlight for a few seconds, he laid it down.

"Okay, I'm ready."

"Those batteries—"

"Dead. That scene we witnessed couldn't have lasted more than two minutes. But it drained the batteries dry."

"Then we're sure of at least one thing. Whatever this operation is, it certainly eats up the juice. . . ."

Outside in the cool darkness Adams lit his pipe and drew on it until the bowl glowed. Bill gave him that leeway, but then he could wait no longer. "What do you think, Professor? What's your opinion? Was that unit merely picking up a signal from some TV station?"

Adams did not answer immediately and Bill began to realize he'd have to learn to wait if he stayed around Neal Adams. Finally, Adams answered Bill's question with one of his own.

"Exactly what did you see in that picture, Bill?"

"It was a war—men fighting."

"True, but what details did you spot?"

"Details? Well, a dozen or so men were fighting their way up that street and a lone defender threw a grenade."

"You're quite correct, but there were a few other things I noticed in passing—rather interesting things. The town itself—New York City."

"It could have been, of course . . ."

"It was. There is only one Empire State Building and it stood clearly in the background. So the battle was taking place in the streets of New York."

"I didn't notice that," Bill murmured.

"I just happened to catch it. But there were other points also—not quite as definite, but still interesting. The soldiers themselves, for instance. We saw them all quite clearly and they had a native look to them. I mean they didn't appear to be invaders."

"There was a definite 'American' look about them."

"The uniforms, too. They were different of course, but the variations weren't of a major character."

"Neither side wore uniforms much different from the regulation Army of today."

"I don't know. We must try to maintain objectivity. It could have been a televised movie. I think, however, we have good grounds to doubt that."

"Then you accept Dad's theory. I mean, your logical reservations are . . ."

Bill's words dribbled away and Adams allowed the silence to stand for a few moments before he answered indirectly.

"I find myself standing in greater awe of your father with every passing moment."

That sudden warmth again! Bill realized he'd found a new world of his own without leaving home. A world of friendship and mutual understanding. Would he ever get used to it?

While he was still searching for words, Neal Adams

came briskly out of his chair, knocking his pipe on its metal arm. "Well, we've done enough for tonight. Let's get some sleep and meet tomorrow with fresh minds."

"Do you suppose those suits really work?"

Then Adams surprised him. "Maybe we ought to put them on and find out. See you tomorrow."

Bill stayed where he was for a while, not rushing in to bed. He was pondering Adams' change of pattern. His stress upon caution and preliminary research had altered somewhat. Had he, too, been caught up in the excitement of this fantastic adventure? That was possible but Bill thought of something else. Adams had acknowledged increasing awe of what he'd discovered. Maybe that indicated a growing confidence.

He's ready to trust Dad and follow him, Bill thought. And his pride made this a thrilling moment.

Trial Run

WHEN NEAL ADAMS returned the next morning, he found Bill where he had left him—in the back yard. But he apparently assumed Bill had not stayed there all night.

"Have a good sleep?" he asked.

"Not too good."

Adams noted Bill's sober expression. "Something wrong?"

"I'm confused."

"Welcome to the club."

Bill kicked restlessly at the grass with the toe of a dirty sneaker. "It hit me last night—all of a sudden—confusion. I guess you could call it doubt."

"That's quite logical."

"You mean . . . doubting?" A faint hostility crept into Bill's tone, as though Adams were condoning disloyalty to his father.

"The letdown. You had a big day yesterday. You hit a high emotional peak. People don't stay on emotional peaks. They slide down again."

"You mean into a depression. But it's not that I feel depressed—"

"Depression can take various forms. You mentioned doubt."

"It's just that . . . well, when I woke up, it all seemed so crazy. Not that I have any doubts about Dad's—"

Adams dropped into a chair and began packing his pipe. "You're trying to be honest with yourself. What's wrong with that?"

"It's this idea about multiple worlds. It was so clear to me yesterday, so simple and logical. But this morning, it doesn't make any sense. It sounds like a—a hodgepodge—crazy—impossible."

"I think I know what you mean. We are conditioned to law and order. Everything under nature's control functions to mathematical perfection. Everything is predictable; the movements of the planets and the movements in an atom. Your father's theory appears to contradict that law and order."

"I guess that's about it. I wish I could express it—how I feel—put it into words."

"I think you're doing pretty well. But there's another way of looking at it. Confusion mounts from lack of understanding." Neal Adams paused to smile. "I'm sure that when you were handed problems in, say trigonometry, they were confusing and made very little sense to you. But when you gained understanding through study, the problems became what they really were, exercises in precise logic. In other words, examples of law and order."

Bill's spirits were rising. He grinned. "Why didn't I think of that?"

Neal Adams' only comment was an answering smile. He was thinking of something else—how quickly Bill responded to an offer of friendship. Adams was forced to admit his one error in seeing Bill as unable to communicate. The lad needed only to be met on his own ground.

Bill was staring at the laboratory, but with his mind obviously elsewhere.

"I thought a lot about Dad and Mom, too," he said. "I recalled something that happened to Dad once. The only time I ever saw him actually frightened. Maybe that's why I remember it."

"He wasn't a man who frightened easily."

"That's right. Anyhow, he and Mother went to Dempsterville one night and drove home late. They used the Belt Parkway and you know how dangerous those turns used to be before they fixed them."

"There were a lot of accidents on that highway."

"Well, Dad came within an inch of going over on one of those hairpin turns. When he got home he told me about it and his hands were shaking. He wasn't scared for himself. It was for Mom. I remember it so clearly that I can quote him. He said, 'My God, Bill! What if I'd gone over and your mother had been killed!' It was the only time . . ."

Momentarily lost in the memory, Bill's voice faded off. He was brought back by Neal Adams' question. "What point are you trying to make, Bill?"

"I'm not sure myself, but I think maybe it isn't all cold science and logic. Emotion—love—they're even more important. I keep remembering his letter. Dad's whole motive for working this theory out was because he lost Mom. He never went off on such wild tangents before."

"I have no doubt that you're right. Hard-headed realists recognize love as one of the greatest driving forces in existence."

Bill grinned and came to his feet. "I guess I just had to get a few things out of my system."

"And now you're ready to carry on?"

"You bet! You didn't forget what you said last night —that we might try out the suits."

"Let's go into the laboratory."

"Try and keep me out," Bill laughed, and ran toward the squat, stone building.

Inside, Neal Adams approached the cabinet-like box they'd previously searched for batteries. "I studied the notes last night," he said, "and beyond all doubt, that has to be your dad's transformer. We'll probably never find out how he got tiny flashlight batteries to contain such tremendous power. But one thing is sure—the power had to be created somehow. He would have drained the whole power plant by merely drawing it through that cable and still would not have had enough."

"So the answer has to be in his transformer," Bill agreed.

"Let's check it again."

To Bill, the interior looked like a big, square container packed by a shipping clerk who liked to twist copper wire into weird shapes. He intimated as much, but just at that moment, Neal Adams found a slot into which two of the small batteries fitted perfectly. He slipped them in and straightened with a look of satisfaction.

"We seem to be on the right track," he said. "Now, while I plug this transformer in, why don't you hunt for your father's supply of batteries? He must have had more than just these and the ones he took with him."

"Okay."

Bill was tingling with excitement, some of it, he knew, was drawn from Neal Adams. Adams was working slowly and speaking in casual, quiet tones. But he was not able to hide the tension underneath. It reflected, if nowhere else, in the narrowing of his eyes and his quick darting glances; also, in the intentness with which he paused to study the notebook he carried.

Bill was back in a very short time. "I've got them. Here in a box. A couple of dozen batteries."

"Good."

"Is there room for more than two in the transformer?"

"There doesn't appear to be. But I think the device on this side is for testing. We'll try it out by checking the ones you found."

"The periscope thing worked for two minutes on the power left in the batteries. How long would you say they would have to supply power for those suits?"

"It's difficult to say. We haven't much to go on. Perhaps the suits need less power to function. Or more, for that matter."

While Adams worked with the transformer, Bill wandered over and began inspecting the suit that lay on the workbench. He fingered the soft plastic material and got an odd reaction. It was difficult to associate the type of travel they contemplated with the suit itself. The clumsily cut garment had none of the "glamour image" that was associated with conveyances of even less fantastic possibilities. It had none of the sleek beauty of a rocket with its nose pointed toward the stars; none of the aura of excitement that surrounded the big missiles poised on their launching pads at Kennedy or any of the other big space projects.

We're out of our minds.

The thought came suddenly and unbidden and Bill rejected it instantly, trying to banish also the twinge of guilt that came with it. The thought automatically embodied lack of faith in his father. He turned and walked quickly back to where Neal Adams was studying a rather crude, handmade dial on the transformer.

"As nearly as I can tell," Adams said, "the *capacity* level on this gauge is marked by a line made with an ordinary lead pencil. If I'm right, all of these batteries are ready for use."

"Then let's get this suspense over with. The suits work or they don't. Let's find out."

"There are a few things we should find out first."

"How long will it take?"

"I don't know. Not too long, I think."

"There's a lot we can never find out except by trying the equipment."

"Quite true, but there's one thing we'd better find out before we start."

"How to work the suits."

"Exactly."

Impatience was pushing Bill. "Let's examine them."

As they walked toward the bench, Adams' attention was on the small battery he carried. "This jacket fooled me. I thought it was zinc. But it isn't. It's plastic. That gives us something to think about."

"What—Neal?" Bill realized this was the first time he'd used Adams' first name. Adams did not seem to mind.

"I examined the suit last night and noticed that there's no metal on that, either. So perhaps metallic substances aren't applicable."

Bill began checking the suit with new interest. It

had some mechanism attached, though not a great deal. There was a small box fastened at the belt that was undoubtedly a rheostat, and a lock-switch on the other side that fitted two small tongues into corresponding holes. But a close examination showed Bill that there was no metal in either unit.

"There's an odd feel to this material," Adams said. "I think maybe it's impregnated with some chemical. Did you ever see your father work with chemicals?"

Bill shook his head. "I don't think so."

"We could soak some out and analyze it, but I don't see much point. I'm more interested in other things. The suits will go on over our regular clothing. I hope it moves everything."

"Everything?"

"It could be embarrassing to land among strangers with nothing on but our skin—unless it turned out to be a nudist world."

"Until we try, we won't even know whether the suit goes with us."

"Or whether we even go ourselves."

Neal had brought another of the four available suits to the bench. He stretched it out and began examining it. "The batteries go into this pocket. They lock into a plastic circuit that includes both controls. Like so. . . ." He completed the power insertion and stepped back.

"Is it ready?"

"As ready as my knowledge and know-how can make it." Adams casually laid down his pipe. "Suppose I put it on and make a test run. If everything works—"

"Not a chance," Bill said resolutely. "Risking the first trial is my job."

"Not necessarily. Suppose we match a coin."

Bill shook his head. "I'm too unlucky."

"All right. Then let's go together."

"It's a deal."

Adams' calm exterior began to shake, his excitement breaking through as he made a final examination of Bill's suit.

"You'd better take all the coins out of your pockets. And anything else of a metallic nature."

Bill complied. "That leaves me seven dollars."

"Which may or may not be of value. Let's climb in."

They began pulling on the suits.

Dressed for the trip they hoped to take, they found themselves looking at each other through plastic windows. Adams signaled to Bill to open the face mask and said, "These suits aren't radio-equipped, so we'll have to work it by signal. I'll tap your shoulder three times. On the third signal, snap your power switch to one and then push your rheostat up to the same capacity." He stopped and looked levelly into Bill's eyes.

"Are you afraid?"

"If you want to know the truth, I'm scared to death."

"So am I. Let's go."

They stood facing each other. Adams raised one

hand and tapped Bill on the shoulder. One tap . . .
two . . . three.

In one motion, they worked the controls on the suits.

Nothing happened. As nearly as either of them could
tell from the hot confines of the suits, absolutely no
changes came about.

After a full minute of waiting, Bill moved a hand
toward the controls, but Adams grasped his wrist and
pulled it away as he shook his head inside the helmet.
Then he opened the face piece.

"Let's not take any chances. It didn't work. That's
what we climbed into these union suits to find out.
So let's climb out again and get back to the drawing
board."

Bill's disappointment was deeper than he'd ever
imagined it could be as he stripped off the suit and
put it back on the bench.

An Unemployed Physicist

"THE ANSWER," NEAL ADAMS SAID, HIS voice reflecting neither satisfaction nor disappointment, "is very simple."

"What is it?" Bill asked, making no effort to hide the way he felt.

"Research, involving hard work and mental sweat."

"I guess that's it."

"We tried the easy way. It didn't work. Now we try the hard way. I'll take this notebook and any other written data we can find and start digging. Gather up every scrap of paper with a marking on it you can find."

There wasn't much. After assembling a pathetically small pile of notes, Bill muttered, "Like I told you, Dad carried most of it in his head."

"Another solid fact we've proved," Adams said cheerfully. "This place has no ventilation and it's beginning to heat up. Let's go over to my place and you can throw dinner together while I start trying to classify this stuff."

"Okay," Bill said. "Maybe I can be of some help by sharpening your pencils and swatting flies."

Outside, Adams headed for the driveway and then stopped dead. "I'd have sworn I drove over, but obviously I didn't."

"I don't remember hearing your motor. But I was out back. It doesn't matter, though. We can use my car."

Neal opened the notebook and was deep in the mysteries of Sam Franklin's personal shorthand when Bill pulled up beside him, having brought his own car from the garage.

Bill was busy pondering their failure. "Maybe we should have checked the suits again. Maybe it was some small thing—the contact points—"

"We'll know more about that by morning. What kind of a cook are you?"

"Very good, if you've got a couple of TV dinners in the freezer."

"Chicken, I think," Neal said absently as he turned a page in the memo book.

He dived into total absorption and Bill had to arouse him when they reached the white bungalow on Faculty Row. "Two TV dinners coming up," he said.

Adams looked up and blinked. "Oh—of course. You got here very quickly."

"It's only four blocks."

Adams continued to study the notes as they went up the walk, climbed the porch stairs, and he pawed blindly for the knob on the screen door. He found it and came out of his preoccupation with a frown.

"I never lock that door."

"Maybe you came out the back."

"I always come out the front."

"You thought you drove over, too. Remember?"

"So I did."

They were turning away to go around the back, when a figure appeared inside; a trim, attractive figure in a flowered dress and a bright apron.

"May I help you gentlemen?"

She had brown hair and was quite pretty. She wore a pleasant smile and the ring on her finger said she was someone's wife.

But what was she doing in Neal Adams' bungalow?

Adams stared at the girl, Bill looked questioningly at Adams, and the girl looked at both of them, still pleasantly, but now a little doubtful.

"Were you looking for someone?"

"I—I thought—" Adams stopped, apparently trying to figure out exactly what he had thought.

"Professor James will be home in half an hour or so," the girl said.

"Professor James?"

"Yes. This is his residence. I'm his wife, Betty."

Neal Adams looked, in obvious confusion, at the two adjoining houses.

"Perhaps you have the wrong address," the girl who called herself Betty James suggested.

"It doesn't seem possible, but . . ."

Evidently working on the belief that a faculty member's wife should be pleasant and co-operative at all times, Betty James asked, "Are you a member of the faculty? I thought I'd met most of the Queens College people."

"Yes . . . I am . . . or was . . . or thought I was . . . or . . ."

Neal Adams had spent most of the time with his mouth open. Now he closed it and appeared to get a grip on himself. "I'm sorry. I'm afraid we *have* made a mistake. Come on, Bill. Let's not bother the lady any further."

He hurried back down the stairs, Bill following. But when he got to the bottom, he turned back. Betty James was still looking out—more doubtfully than ever now—from behind the screen.

"I beg your pardon," Adams said, "but just one question since you've been so pleasant about this rude intrusion. How long has Professor James been at Queens College?"

"Almost eleven months now. He gave up a post at Ohio State to come here and take over when—"

Neal Adams did not wait. "Thank you very much," he said quickly and hurried out to the car. He was in the seat staring straight ahead when Bill climbed in behind the wheel.

Bill rolled the car on down the street and turned the first available corner. When they were out of sight of the bungalow, he braked to a halt.

"I got lost somewhere along the line," he said. "Can you tell me what that was all about? Since when has somebody named James moved into your bungalow."

"Not only into my bungalow, but into my job. I'm unemployed as of the present moment."

"I don't get it. Has everyone gone crazy?

"I can't give authoritative data on that, but this I know: Eleven months ago I almost left Queens College to take a job in private industry. I went so far as to submit my resignation. Then I changed my mind. I asked myself what I needed all that money for, and took my old job back."

Their heads turned simultaneously and they stared at each other as the same thoughts went through their minds. Then Bill put his attention back on the road and the car moved slowly forward.

"What's your immediate reaction?" Neal Adams asked.

"I—I can't put it into words yet."

"It occurs to me that the first mark on those control knobs we turned represents about a year."

"It worked after all," Bill muttered in awe.

"It certainly did."

"But nothing has changed for me. This is no different than my other world."

"Perhaps you're a little more reckless," Neal said dryly. "There was a red light back there. You went through it."

"I did?" Bill said. "I'll have to watch that."

They were approaching a corner. "Shall we go back to the laboratory and climb into those suits before they come and slap a ticket on your car?"

"It might be a good idea," Neal said.

Bill had gone somewhat out of their way. Now, turning back, they found they had some ten blocks to go. "This is kind of a weird experience," Bill said. "Looking at a world that isn't your own and trying to find out how it's different."

"It probably isn't different at all. My quitting my job or not wouldn't affect the town."

"But it did," Bill said as he pointed. "That used to be Elkin's Drug Store on that corner. Now it's a gas station."

Neal Adams' brow was furrowed in thought. "That might give us another clue."

"What clue?"

"Even with some law of probability functioning, there's got to be a catalyst, a cause for movement, a governing action of some sort, to create a world, or change a world in some aspects and allow it to function as two worlds."

"You lost me," Bill said.

"I don't think my taking or not taking a job would be enough in itself to change a fixed pattern. So perhaps the probabilities of individuals have to coincide."

Bill jerked his head to the left. "That place there was Arnold's Supermart. Now it's a theater."

"Of course! It's an acceptable step ahead in our groping. At the time I was on the verge of two possibilities, the same situation existed for those two people. And probably for others. The combined impetus created the new world. If the number of possibilities hadn't been great enough—just my own, for instance—nothing would have happened. No new world would have been created."

"It's as good an idea as any," Bill admitted.

"It has to be that way. If a new world originated on the basis of every human possibility, we'd have a vast chaos."

"How do you know we haven't?"

"There is absolute law and perfect order in the cosmic plan. You can be sure of that."

"I'm getting pretty confused," Bill admitted.

"That's natural. But you ought to be very proud at seeing your father's theories turned into fact."

"I am, of course. But it will take a little getting used to. Another thing that's got me scared, now. How

are we possibly going to find my father in all those
multiple worlds?"

"It does sound difficult, but again we have logic to
fall back on."

Bill grinned bravely. "Mine's so full of holes, I keep
falling through."

"Maybe mine is full of holes too, but I'm sure that
your father wouldn't have gone off on his journey
without having some idea of where he should go."

"In what world, you mean?"

"Yes. We're merely blundering around in areas he
studied thoroughly. And until it's proven otherwise,
let's assume we will find a way to follow him with
some degree of intelligence."

Bill straightened his shoulders. "We'll find him."

"Of course. And think of this fantastic experience,
Bill. Your father has made it possible for us to go
where no other beings ever went before."

Adams spoke heartily in order to help Bill lift his
spirits, and a few minutes later the car came to a halt
in the driveway of the Franklin house.

Bill stared at it as he got out. "This place stayed
the same in both worlds."

"There was no reason why it should change. But
another thing occurs to me now. We could have known
the truth without leaving the laboratory."

"How?"

"The coins and metal objects we left on the bench.
We didn't look for them when we took the suits off.

A search would have shown them to be missing, I'm sure."

A blank look came on Adams' face as he finished speaking. His mouth and jaws began twisting as though he were in pain.

"What's the matter?" Bill asked.

Adams laughed. "We didn't even need the coins. All I had to do was to put my tongue in the right place. I had a big filling in one of my upper right molars. It had a metal filling. Now there's nothing but a hole there."

Bill began moving his own tongue around. "I've got fillings too, but they're all there."

"Then they're made of plastic."

They went directly to the laboratory where Neal Adams began examining the periscope device. He said, "I'm wondering about the sequence in which your father worked."

"What do you mean?"

"I'd like to know whether this scanner came before or after the suits."

"What difference would it make?"

"It would indicate a trend in your father's thinking and might give us some clues."

"I don't see how."

"If he built this scanner first, it would indicate that he found the other worlds as a result of it and then built the suits as a means of reaching them."

"But if the suits came first?"

"Then, it seems to me, he wouldn't have bothered

with the scanner—wouldn't have taken the time. He would have put a suit to use and gone out to see for himself."

"I still don't get what you're driving at," Bill said.

"Only this—that in order to make the transitions properly, the suits and the scanner may work as a unit. Perhaps the scanner is some sort of a steering device."

"But we've made a transition without it."

"That's true, but without any notion of where we were going. If we were mariners using that system, we could circle around in the middle of the ocean until our ship rotted."

"But how would we go about using the scanner and the suits as a unit?"

"We could at least re-examine them with that idea in mind."

Then the enormity, the vast impossibility of the whole idea suddenly struck Bill forcibly. He passed a hand across his face in a gesture of confusion.

"Neal! All of a sudden this seems so crazy." He looked around as though he'd never seen the laboratory before. "This place—this shop. It's the same as it always was and yet it doesn't seem real!"

"I get the same impression, but I think I have an explanation."

"I'd like to hear it."

"First, let's see if we can't restore your confidence with a little logic. We've got to see your father in one of two ways—he was either an incredibly brilliant man or he was insane. He either knew what he was doing or he had a crazy idea and therefore belonged in a mental hospital."

Bill flared. "Do you think Dad was insane? If you do—"

"I asked you what you thought."

"He was one of the most brilliant scientists that ever lived."

"All right. I've gone along with you, haven't I? That should indicate my belief. And so long as we both see him in that light, we'd better concede that he has a solid explanation for what appears to be crazy to us."

Bill's lips bent into a smile that was strictly from tension. "You're saying we'd better believe that or abandon the whole project."

"We can't abandon it, Bill." Neal Adams spoke quietly, but there was an undertone of deepest seriousness in his voice. "Not only that, but we've got to go on—and quickly."

"What on earth do you mean?"

"I mean that we can't go back. I'm almost certain of that. And we have to go on because I've got a hunch this world we're in could disappear at any moment."

Bill's confusion became even more apparent. He reached out and laid his hand on the bench as though to assure himself that it still existed.

"We can't go back, Bill," Neal Adams repeated. "We can only move ahead."

The Uncertain Worlds of Maybe

BILL WAS DEEPLY ASHAMED OF HIM-
self for his childish actions. Neal Adams' reminder
that the strongest people sometimes react sharply to
continued pressure was of no comfort.

Bill in turn had reminded Neal that he himself had
not given in to pressure, bringing a smile from the
physicist.

"Maybe I'm not smart enough to know when the
pressure is on," he'd said.

After that they'd gotten down to business and Neal

had explained his startling statements. Then Neal had gone to work on the problem of integrating the suits and the scanner and Bill had started pacing the floor while he digested the flood of new theories Neal had given him; theories they would have to accept as fact until proven otherwise.

The danger of their present situation was based on Neal's idea of comparatives. He believed that worlds springing from minor possibilities were minor and unstable worlds. As he explained it, "Whether I kept my job at the college or left it made little difference in the general scheme of things. Coupled with a few other individualized possibilities, it did create another world. But with little that was different or of any great consequence, that world—the one we're in now —will probably not be sustained and will vanish. I have no idea where that would leave you and me, and I'd rather not stay to find out."

As to the one-way trip they were taking, "We can't base a whole theory on it of course, but we've found nothing of a reversible nature on the suits or the scanner. All the controls are plus. There are no minuses. Everything positive. Nothing negative. So I'm very much afraid, Bill, that we can't go home again."

The news hadn't been as frightening as might have been expected. After Bill regained his poise and balance, he saw both points almost as abstracts. The thought had come: Dad is out there somewhere. What applies to me applies to him. If we're in the same boat, that's fine with me.

It *was* a little unnerving to pace a floor that might vanish at any moment, so when Neal straightened from bending over the scanner and cried, "I think we've taken a giant step!" Bill rushed to his side.

"These screws. I thought they merely held the cover-plate down. But they're controls. Imagine guiding yourself from world to world with an ordinary screw-driver."

"Dad never was much for frills. He saw everything as strictly functional."

"He proved that by making gauge points with an ordinary lead pencil. "Now—watch the scanner. If I'm right, we're going to do some armchair traveling."

As Bill watched the plate his fists were doubled from the excitement.

"The images will be a little more disciplined this time," Neal said. "If I'm working this thing right, we'll go back to that second war between the States."

The image came in. It was the same street they'd seen previously, but hostilities had ceased. Soldiers in the familiar, yet unfamiliar uniforms, were lounging around in various states of ease.

"The question is," Neal said, "who occupies New York City in that world, the North or the South?"

"If we had sound we could listen in to what they're saying. A few *you-alls* and I'd bet on the South."

Neal reached toward the controls. "We have to remember that there is no time span involved. These are all worlds of this exact moment."

"Have you any idea what controls the location of the image?"

"You mean, is it stationary?"

"Yes. Are we always going to see that same street in New York City?"

"I think not." Neal touched another of the screws. The image flickered and they were viewing the Statue of Liberty with Staten Island in the background.

"The location control is highly sensitive and quite intricate. I can move the picture around, but I haven't the least idea of how to direct it. What comes up is pure chance."

As they watched an overhead car shot into view. "Look," Bill cried, "they've run a monorail from Manhattan to Staten Island."

"It would seem that they advanced in transportation."

"I'd certainly like to know who's winning the war."

"Whichever way it goes," Neal said, "I think we're looking at one of the stable worlds. The possibility-components involved are vast. They affect millions of people."

"I wonder how many stable worlds there are?"

"In comparative terms, they must be far fewer than the unstable ones. We might think of them in the same terms as solid stars in a galaxy composed mainly of dust and small asteroids. The dust and the asteroids would be the unstable worlds. Would you like to watch a few of them?"

"I sure would!" Bill's eyes were alive with excitement. "Boy! You've got that scanner performing like a trained seal."

Neal was applying two screwdrivers now. "The only difference," he observed, "is that a trained seal functions on a couple of fish. This mechanism eats up enough power to light a fair-sized city."

They were silent now, both staring at the screen.

"It's like a montage," Bill murmured.

"That's an apt description."

And it was, except there is usually a pattern of some sort to a montage. Here there was no pattern. Scenes of cities, oceans, mountains, and plains faded in and out. Some were mere flashes of images that appeared and vanished instantly. Others lingered for a few seconds. Some remained to form a backdrop of the even more unstable worlds that flashed and faded against them.

"I see what you mean," Bill marveled.

"The ones that appear only for seconds are worlds based on the slimmest of possibilities and have only the slightest of effect quotient. The ones that remain longer expand in ratio on both counts."

"The one we're in now is pretty stable in relation to those."

"It had to be or we couldn't have landed here. Evidently a great many small probabilities meshed in the time cycle to operate it. But I think it's far from stable because there isn't enough of an effect quotient in it."

Bill's spirits were again high. He grinned. "Then let's get out of it."

"You haven't forgotten that we can't come back?"

"I haven't forgotten, but I wanted to ask you—are you absolutely certain of that? Maybe if we find Dad, he has a way."

"There's one thing you may have overlooked that just about clinches the no-return factor, I think."

"What's that?"

"The battery recharger stays where it is. It's constructed of metal. So regardless of everything else, we stay in whatever world we're in when the batteries give out."

"Have you figured out how long they'll last?"

"With the supply we have on hand, I can only say quite a while. We won't know for sure, of course, until we make an actual test."

"That will be when the ones we're using run out."

"That's right. Then we'll have an absolute to go by, provided they're fully charged when we start."

"The ones we used to come to this world are in the charger right now. They should be ready."

"Then I don't see where we've got any problems at all."

"That's certainly a novel outlook," Neal said.

"A problem is something you have to make a decision about, so figure it out. We don't have to decide whether or not to go back because we can't *get* back.

We don't have to decide if we want to stay here because *here* isn't going to be around much longer. So
we have no choice but to go ahead."

Neal smiled. "I bow to your supreme logic. Now
let's see if we can apply a little of it to finding the
world your father is in. First, we mustn't, under any
circumstance, overshoot it because we can't go back.
Do you think there is any pattern or sequence to
the stable worlds? I suspect there is. I've scanned them
in the same order three times."

"That should help some, but worlds are big places."

"You mean it might be easy to miss meeting your
father even if we hit his world?"

"Yes."

"We can only hope for a break. One thing, though.
He arrived in whatever world he went to on this exact
spot. So at least we'll find a place he's been."

"If that's true," Bill asked, "why is the scanner
beamed on New York City? This spot certainly
couldn't have become New York in any sane world."

Neal shrugged. "The scanner is certainly more
flexible."

Bill snapped his fingers as a thought occurred.
"Hey! There's something else. This spot doesn't necessarily have to be the same in other worlds. It could
be—well, anything. Suppose we land in a hundred
feet of water."

"Then we'll get wet," Neal shrugged.

"Or suppose a stable probability promoted a new
ice age. We might arrive in the center of an iceberg."

"We can't take an ice pick with us. Metal won't make the trip."

"That's what I like about you," Bill said, "You've got all the answers."

"And what I like about you is that you're always so optimistic."

But they were both grinning, proof that their morale was high. Making an oblique comment on this, Neal said, "I think knowing the percentages—knowing what we're up against—is the big difference. It's the not knowing that rips a man's nerves."

"I guess so. But standing here in a world that may disappear before I can get that suit on isn't helping my nerves a bit."

"Then get it on."

As Bill stepped into the bulky garment and pulled it up, Neal went through a ritual Bill hadn't seen before. He picked up an extension cord and plugged it into the back of the scanner. Then he plugged the other end in a receiving block between the shoulders that Bill had overlooked.

"The suits and the scanner are synchronized," Neal said, "and the scanner is calibrated to a 'jump' pattern. That's the only term I can think of that seems to describe it. If I'm right, the scanner will go with us."

"What does it do?"

"It lands us in worlds of a minimum stability-quotient. That means we don't go out and get mixed up in that montage."

"But even unstable worlds hold us up. This one did."

"I agree that there's always the danger of landing in an apparently stable world that's about to fade out. But we'll have to take our chances on that."

"Then let's get with it. Something tells me the floor is getting soft."

"Okay. Get ready to man your controls. Three taps on the shoulder."

"Right," Bill answered, his smile tight. "Good luck to—*us!*"

The War of the States

BILL CAME TO WITH A SENSE OF COM-plete separation from anything he had ever done, any place he had ever known—or for that matter, anyone he had ever been.

Seeking, with his first wisp of returning conscious-ness, an identification, he recalled a name and a place. Bill Franklin. Queen City.

But was it accurate? He wasn't sure.

The situation and the place of the moment became more pressing questions.

Then everything came back with startling clarity.

There had been no interim between this world and the one he and Neal had left. Rather, an instantaneous transition. The walls of the laboratory had faded to the accompaniment of gunfire. There was the close crackle of small arms with the deeper thunder of far-off artillery behind it.

Then it was as though the chairs they'd been sitting on were yanked out from under them and they tumbled to the floor. But not to the floor; to the ground in a forest where a heavy padding of dead leaves broke their fall and the extension cords from the scanner kept them from rolling down into a ravine.

Neal's mind clicked first. "Good lord!" he exclaimed. "We've popped up in the middle of a battle!"

At that moment, a rattle of rifle slugs could be heard, and a series of hoarse, unintelligible commands were barked out from somewhere nearby.

"It looks as though we didn't get the scanner clear of the war," Neal said.

With a major effort of his will, Bill cleared his mind of the sudden panic. He followed Neal's example and disconnected himself from the scanner.

They were against a rock cluster in a partially wooded area, and had arrived in the midst of a battle indeed. As they crouched down beside the scanner, a sweep of running men appeared. They were easily identified from the New York City street battle that Neal and Bill had tuned in on the scanner at the laboratory. Armed with light machine guns, they were moving fast and paid no attention to the two visitors from another world.

The camouflaging effect of the rocks may have helped in this respect, the spaces having the same gray, neutral coloring.

The squad had evidently blundered into an ambush of some sort and was in full retreat.

"I wonder if they're North or South?" Bill said.

"I don't think it matters much at the moment. Get that plug back in. We're leaving."

The men continued to stream by as Bill obeyed Neal's order and reached for his scanner cord. But he had flung it away as he'd dived for the shelter of the rocks and now the plug was caught in the roots of a bush. Bill tried to flip it loose as the last of the fleeing contingent went out of sight.

"Hurry up," Neal snapped. "Get that plug in!"

But it was too late. A pursuing force came into view and half a dozen soldiers cut away from the main stream to surround the rock cluster.

A command was barked. "Hold it, buster!"

Bill froze with his hand extended, whereupon, the soldier scowled, pushed back his helmet, and scratched his head. "A couple of deep-sea divers. But what the devil are they doing here?" He turned his eyes to a comrade. "What do you think, Sarge?"

The soldier called Sarge, obviously the leader of the squad, scratched his head also. "Espionage, I guess." He loosed a squirt of tobacco juice at a bug near his foot and drowned the poor insect.

One of the soldiers extended his gun and poked at the scanner in gingerly fashion. "Some kind of a bomb, maybe?" he muttered.

The sergeant did not seem to think so, however. He was studying Bill and Neal with alert bemusement.

"What kind of outfits are those?" he asked of no one in particular. And, quite logically, no one answered. He moved two steps closer and touched Neal's shoulder with the snout of his rifle. "You—buster—what's your outfit?"

"Intelligence," Neal snapped. "Special duty. Turn that blasted gun the other way."

"Special duty in the middle of a battle zone? You must be off your rocker. Let's see your papers."

Neal's scowl matched that of the sergeant and Bill was filled with admiration for this magnificent bluff. At the same time, he realized how it would have sounded if he or Neal had said, Pardon us, fellows, but we just dropped in from another world. Go right on with what you're doing. Don't mind us.

And it was very strange because, even while he should have been thoroughly frightened, he had a hard time keeping a grin off his face.

The sergeant's scowl deepened as he continued to study his two strange prisoners. He cocked his head as the soldier next to him said, "Sarge, why don't you ask 'em Intelligence North or Intelligence South?"

Neal, simulating anger, dropped his arms. "This is nonsense, Sergeant. Either leave us to our work or take us to headquarters."

"Leave you here, buster? That'll be the day!"

The squad had gathered curiously around the scanner. Neal turned on them angrily. "Don't touch that unit, you men! It contains delicate mechanism!"

Bill moved up beside him. He realized Neal's sole purpose was to stall for time and hope for some kind of a break. He added his own scowl to the act but underneath he was accusing himself of cowardice for running to cover.

The sergeant had removed his helmet and was again scratching his closely clipped skull. "I don't get it," he said to the soldier beside him. "This sector was sealed off tight. How'd they get in with that gadget on their backs?"

"Air drop?" the soldier asked.

"Are you kidding?" A pigeon with a cracker in its beak would have drawn a missile."

The sergeant's quandary was apparent. If Neal and Bill were Intelligence from his own army, he might get into trouble if he treated them like prisoners. But if they were the enemy, who could tell what kind of a caper this was?

Bill could almost hear the wheels going around in the sergeant's head as he grappled with the problem. Then too, it was obvious that the squad was out of communication with their command post. Perhaps the type of operation demanded this. But regardless, it complicated the sergeant's problem.

The soldiers had stepped back from the scanner and Neal bent over and picked up one of the extension cords. He turned to the sergeant. "You have a right to be suspicious, I guess. So let me put you in touch with headquarters. That ought to satisfy you."

"You can talk over that thing?"

"Of course. We'll plug in our mikes."

Bill understood now. Neal was going to try and escape into another world, and Bill, in answer to Neal's gesture, turned his back in order to be plugged in.

"Hold it!"

The barked command stopped Neal cold. It came from the sergeant who had raised his automatic rifle. Evidently the sergeant was a man slow to make up his mind. But when he did arrive at a decision, he was definite about it. He was very definite about this one.

"We'll check it out at the command post. Pick up that gadget, men. You guys fall in and keep your hands high."

Neal's plan had had only one thing wrong with it. It had failed. He and Bill fell in behind the other two prisoners and the march began.

As they moved forward, Neal fell back a step from the prisoners ahead and risked a try at whispered conversation. "Things look bad. We can only keep our eyes open and play it by ear."

"Your trick almost worked," Bill said.

"Close doesn't count, I'm afraid."

"One thing—I'm getting pretty tried of this war. I wish someone would win and get it over with."

"I'm with you on that," Neal replied.

"I wonder who's winning?"

"I'd like to know which side captured us. But asking would have sounded pretty silly."

"I'd say the North. These boys haven't got a Southern accent among them. But we'll find out at the command post."

"I don't know," Neal whispered grimly. "But I'll bet we won't find any roses scattered in our path."

"Shut up, you two!"

The command was barked by the sergeant and after that the column moved in silence.

The command post had been set down hastily in a thicker part of the forest. Neal and Bill were brought before a weary-looking captain who glared at them across a small wooden table.

"Who are these two clowns?" he demanded.

"We picked them up in a skirmish over in Red Sector, sir," the sergeant reported. "They claim they're from Intelligence."

"I wouldn't doubt it," the captain replied with some bitterness. "The kind of stuff they've been sending us must come from idiots running around in masquerade getups." But he was making a tired joke. He obviously did not believe the Intelligence story.

The scanner had been brought in and placed beside the table. The captain eyed it distastefully. "You mean they were running around in the woods with that thing?"

"Yes, sir."

"What is it?"

"I don't know, sir."

"I'd say it might be built to scare fish with, but they aren't near any water."

"They offered to call headquarters on it for me."

"Whose headquarters?"

"I don't know, sir."

Neal was following the conversation closely, but Bill scarcely heard it. His eye was on the heavy black automatic pistol that had been dropped carelessly on one end of the table. The longer he looked at the gun, the better he liked a desperate plan that had come into his mind. There was no one close by except the captain and the sergeant. Both of them looked very tired. Neither was at all alert. So if he grabbed the gun he might be able to cover them and hold them at bay— hostages so to speak—while he and Neal plugged in the scanner and left for some other world.

The captain's head was turned away, his attention on the scanner.

Bill tensed his muscles and lunged for the gun. He got it into his hands and almost raised it.

But the sergeant evidently was not as tired as he'd appeared to be. And his apparent nonalertness must have been an illusion because he moved like a rocket fired off a launching pad. His doubled fist rose and fell like a hammer and this worst of all possible worlds vanished along with Bill's consciousness. . . .

And now he was coming to. He opened his eyes and found himself in what was evidently a hastily erected prefab hut with no floor in it. Nor was he alone. Neal and two uniformed prisoners made it a foursome.

Bill sat up. "What happened?"

"You missed," Neal said.

Bill shook his head. The movement was painful. "It was a fool play."

"Certainly—because it failed. If you'd succeeded it would have been a brilliant play. That's how things go in wartime."

The two uniformed prisoners were more friendly than hostile and definitely curious. They looked to Bill to be in their mid-twenties and didn't seem particularly frightened.

The handsome blond youth seemed to be the spokesman for the pair. He was regarding Bill with frank curiosity. "You got a real good whack, friend."

"I thought a tree fell on me," Bill groaned.

"Who are you guys, anyhow? What are you made up for?" The blond youth had a Southern accent that would have been pleasant to listen to under other circumstances.

Bill had his head cradled in both hands. He was massaging it gently. He moved it just enough to indicate Neal "Who did he tell you we were?"

"Why, he's a real joker, he is. He said you're a couple of butterfly salesmen out collecting stock. But you know something? I just didn't believe that nohow." The blond youth seemed quite amused—as though he enjoyed a good gag as well as the next man.

Bill closed his eyes and tried to orientate his groggy

mind. But then it worked with passable efficiency because it suggested a possible way to get a little information.

"I think that guy knocked a few brain cells loose. I'm not sure I know who I am. Or where I am. Where are we, anyhow?"

"Why, friend, you been picked up by a Yankee advance unit. They come down here to probe our defenses."

"Who's fighting who?"

"Why, the North and the South, friend. Ain't you been reading the papers?"

"I know that. But who's winning?"

"Now who do you suppose?"

"A fine mess to stumble into."

"Like I said, friend," the blond youth went on. "You been picked up by a Yank and I think they're going to shoot you two for you grabbin' at the captain's automatic. He don't like for folks to go 'round snatchin' at his weapons. So guess he'll just shoot you two."

"Why are we in here then? Why don't they get it over with?"

"I got a kind of hunch that Yank captain just don't want to make no mistake when it ain't necessary. He probably checked with his battalion headquarters and told them to check this Intelligence thing you tossed at him."

"Then he really isn't sure."

"Oh, he's sure all right. But like I said, he figures

there's no point in making any mistakes he don't have to."

"What about you two?"

"Oh, we're not going to get shot. We're prisoners of war. He thinks he's going to take us back with him."

"He *thinks?*"

The youth leaned closer, his expression more friendly now. "Uh-huh. And I forgot to tell you. He just *thinks* he's going to shoot you guys."

"What's to stop him?"

"Unless I'm way off," the blond youth whispered, "there's going to be a lot of excitement out there pretty soon now. The captain thinks he moved real quiet, but he didn't. He's got big feet and his shoes squeak. Why, they heard him clumping along clear down in Mobile!"

As though the words had been a signal, gunfire broke out on all sides of the prefab hut. There were sudden shouts and sounds of rapid movement outside.

"They'll be outnumbered forty to one," the blond youth exulted as he arose and hit the door with his shoulder.

The door was surprisingly stubborn for such a fragile looking prefab. While the action moved swiftly past outside, the two uniformed prisoners hit the door in concert. It gave on the fourth assault and they tumbled out into the open.

Neal went to the door and looked out. After a quick check, he motioned Bill forward. "They don't care about us," he said. "The action went by and they followed it. We may have a couple of God-given minutes."

He ran toward the captain's table. It was deserted. The assignment of the Northern unit had obviously not been to stand and fight a superior force. They had vanished like smoke.

"Come on," Neal urged. "We may have time to make it. But we'll have to hurry. They'll be back and the Southerners will be just as stuffy about things as the Northerners were."

They reached the table and found the scanner apparently untouched. They plugged each other in. As they pawed desperately at their controls, there was a shout from the returning troops and slugs thudded into the table.

They threw their switches and jammed the rheostats full on.

One-World Theory

IT WAS PITCH-DARK, THE BLACK-
ness coming with that weird abruptness they had experienced before; but more startling this time because
the night around them was like a trap.

"I hope it's only night," Neal said.

"Maybe it's the bottom of a well," Bill retorted.

"I don't feel any walls."

"And this is grass under us. There's a breeze, too."

"The best thing to do is peel out of these suits and
wait."

"We don't seem to be in any danger," Bill observed. "At least none that we can see."

"Then why don't you try to get a little sleep?"

"I'm wide awake."

"Quite logical, after the racket we just escaped."

They were silent for a time. Then Bill said, "It's pretty discouraging."

"We got clear. We got away alive and in one piece —I mean two pieces."

Bill did not even smile there in the pitch-black. "I mean about finding Dad. I'm beginning to think it's like hunting for the right grain of sand on a beach."

"Getting that impression is not difficult. But remember the mathematical problem we discussed back at your house. First there is the confusion of facing the problem itself. And if it happens to be a difficult one, the confusion and apparent difficulty increases as you dig into it."

"But this—"

"This is no different. Simpler in fact, in that our difficulties haven't really increased. They are about the same as when we started."

Bill laughed. "You have a way of simplifying things."

"Perhaps oversimplifying them. But I've been doing a lot of thinking about your father's theory."

"Have you found holes in it?"

"It isn't a matter of finding holes. It is more trying to follow along behind him and fill the gaps that come from our lack of knowledge."

"Have you found any answers?"

"I've come to a conclusion. I think that in truth, there is only one world with many phases."

"But we've already seen others!"

"Have we? I'm not sure. We know this—that Nature experiments a great deal. We saw indisputable evidence of that in the world into which we were born. Life was introduced on earth in its most primitive forms. Then, over eons and ages, Nature experimented. The life forms improved and became more complicated. There is evidence that Nature even made mistakes. She shaped life forms, tried them out, and then discarded them. But all the time, her objective was obvious—to improve, to refine, to develop ever better structures."

"I can follow that," Bill said, "but I don't see quite where you're trying to lead me."

"Well, the things I've spoken of were still all in one world—right?"

Bill nodded, forgetting that Neal couldn't see him. In a few moments, Neal went on.

"We know that because there, we were in a position to grasp them and fit them into their proper dimensions. We could see earth turn from a ball of hot lava into a fertile planet. We could watch the dinosaurs, the huge life forms, develop, fail to fit into the great plan, and vanish."

"The dinosaur was a mistake of nature, then?"

"We can as well call it that as anything else."

"And a lot of other forms that didn't . . ."

"There were many. But to go on—this theory of

your father's that obviously has substance. Can't we classify it in the same manner? Why shouldn't we call it a broader, more complicated process of the same nature; a less comprehensible one, true, but that comes about through our lack of mental scope. It's merely more difficult to see."

"That does change the picture a little," Bill admitted.

"It changes it a great deal. It simplifies the whole problem."

"Not a million worlds, but just one," Bill mused. "Then that means, all the worlds are only paths leading in the same direction."

"And, if the theory is correct, ending up in the same place."

"Then all we're doing is heading back to the same world we left."

"Or perhaps we never left it."

A new enthusiasm came into Bill's voice as he said, "Concepts are funny things. You start rolling things around in your mind and you can come up with the darndest pictures!"

"That's what your mind is for—to shape new pictures."

"It's like coming home, for instance. Let's say home is the world and I'm on the other side of town. There are ten different streets I can take to get there and all of them are different. I can go through a residential section, or the downtown section, or the warehouse section."

"That's right, but let's say you're lost and all anyone can tell you is the right direction."

"And that's kind of what's happened to us! We were lost and Dad gave us the general direction. So all we have to do is keep going."

"It would seem to me," Neal said, "that this was the key structure of his theory."

"Maybe it's a brand new angle even he didn't think of."

"I doubt it, because he apparently was very sure he would eventually find what he was looking for, so he must have known he would come finally to the true, perfected world. I doubt if even he could have solved the maze we originally visualized."

"A world perfected by many experiments!" Bill cried. "It's so simple when you think it out!"

Neal's chuckle came through the darkness. "But there is one thing you must remember."

"What's that?"

"We could be dead wrong. That's another thing about theories. Just as with problems, you can't be sure until you have the answer."

"Then let's go find it. What are we waiting for? Let's move on. I want to find Dad."

"Maybe," Neal gently reminded, "it's just a matter of waiting for sunrise."

"You mean—golly! Maybe this *is* the place!"

"Don't raise your hopes too high. But at the same time it makes sense to wait and find out."

"I wonder what time it is?"

"I don't think it will be long. Things seem to be turning gray."

They had peeled off their cumbersome suits and found the breeze to be of an ideal temperature, around seventy, Neal had guessed. The grass under them had tended to indicate a country setting. But they could only wait to find out.

Quickly now, the blackness became diluted with gray, and a horizon, now dotted with dark shadows which became trees, proved that they were facing the east.

Next, they discovered that they were sitting in the open, in a richly sodded area of what seemed to be a park. Color began appearing now, tended flower beds, and obvious signs of landscaping.

"Maybe this *is* it!" Bill whispered, his hopes rising to a high crest. "It's certainly a civilized world."

"All the same," Neal replied, "I suggest caution. Let's crawl into that bank of bushes over there and do a little watching before we go out to meet the people."

"But the place looks so peaceful."

"Most places do when there's no one around. But somebody might turn up."

They moved through the cool dawn toward the bushes, lugging the scanner with them, and settled down to wait. The world around them brightened.

"I feel like a duck hunter in a blind," Bill said.

Neal frowned and stirred uneasily. "I wish plastic

guns had been invented before we left Queens College."

"Do you think we'll need weapons?"

"I don't know. It's just a feeling I have. Let's stay alert."

The sunrise was quite normal. So were the colors around them. The grass was a lush green, and the blossoms in the flower beds were familiar.

"Tulips over there," Neal said.

"And a row of lilac bushes just starting to bloom."

But at that point, all semblance of normality vanished. There came the sound of heavy footsteps—slow, lumbering. They turned their eyes in that direction. They waited, then stared in dumbfounded amazement.

"It's a zoo!" Bill whispered.

"Maybe," Neal replied under his breath, "but not like any we've ever been in before."

They were silent now as the footsteps approached, passed them, and moved on. The footsteps died. They stared at each other.

Bill spoke first. "Did you see what I saw?"

Neal, no less stunned for all his more adult poise, replied, "I guess I did. What else was there?"

"Nothing but an ape—"

"Riding a small dinosaur—"

"With a saddle—"

"And a bridle—"

"And dressed like a man going to work!"

Simian World

THEY WERE IN A PARK, but what they could see beyond did not resemble a modern city. But yet, somehow it did.

"A civilization gone wrong," Bill muttered.

"Not exactly," Neal replied. "What we have to do is accept what we've seen as reality here. Then things will become more logical. It is here. Therefore, somehow, it fits in."

What they'd seen and were still seeing was difficult to accept.

"Apes acting like people," Bill said. "Do *you* accept it?"

"I see it. Therefore I have to."

Remaining where they were, they had continued to peer out. The incredible ape populace was going to work. Somewhere along the line of this fantastic evolution, they had acquired a sense of modesty. They wore clothing. Also, they were far more erect specimens than Neal and Bill had known in the zoos and circuses of their native world.

"You've heard it said, no doubt," Neal whispered, "that if the ape had a well-developed thumb it would rule the world."

"Do you mean, in this world it was given a thumb?"

"Not just the ape. I've seen baboons, chimpanzees, gorillas—just about every species—"

"The monkey world. It's crazy."

"They're all here."

Neal's amazement was fast being replaced by sheer interest in what he saw as a fantastic phenomenon.

"We're lucky," he said, "in landing at this spot."

"Lucky?" asked Bill. "I don't quite see how—"

"I mean, it's a perfect observation post. We can discover a great deal about them from where we sit."

"They've learned to weave cloth and sew it into clothing."

"But mechanically, they failed."

"What makes you say that?"

"There aren't any mechanical means of transportation. Not even bicycles."

"They ride those funny-looking dinos and bronts. The birds are even—well, crude looking."

"On the face of it, that doesn't appear to make sense."

"It sure doesn't. The dinos and their relatives died out ages before the monks came along."

"That's just another readjustment we have to make in our thinking," Neal said. "This must be the merging of two seemingly unrelated possibilities—the one in which the big beasts didn't die out, and the world in which nature experimented by developing the simians into more capable living mechanisms."

"I guess seeing is believing," Bill grumbled, "but my toughest adjustment is in believing what I see."

"Maybe I can help you there, too," Neal offered. "Suppose an observer had spent time only with the prehistoric cave man and then was suddenly catapulted into the modern world—the world we left. He would see that later version of *homo sapiens* obviously sprang from the cave men he'd known, but he'd still have a hard time believing it."

"I guess that's right."

"The variations in this civilization are fascinating," Neal went on. "For instance, have you looked closely at those houses over there? I have an idea there are no stairways in them. And probably no inside rooms."

Bill studied the structures while an ugly leathery-looking little bird perched on an overhead tree and squalled at them.

"The larger openings in the walls seem to be doors,"

Bill said. "And you'll notice that a pole reaches up to every one of them."

"Then that's the way they get into their homes—up the poles. I wonder why they didn't build houses with doors that close, and stairways, the way we do?"

"It would appear that they retained the basic instincts of their ancestors and refined upon them. The closed dwelling place is logical to us. Our ancestors lived in caves. But the monkeys went into the trees ages ago. And their hides haven't lost the protective hair so far as I can see, therefore shelter from the cold isn't a problem."

"And so their dwellings here are refinements of tree houses—living in trees."

"That seems to be the situation."

"With no cars or wagons, they don't need wide streets. That's why the houses are so close together. I wonder if they've invented the wheel."

"I'm sure they have. They couldn't have come this far without it. They certainly have tools. They shape wood and build their houses."

"Also," Neal added, "they've developed a sense of order and beauty. "I'd give a lot to know what form of government they have."

"I'd just as soon not find out," Bill said, "Do you think we can wriggle into our suits and get out of here without being spotted?"

"I'd like to stay around a while."

"They'd probably kill us."

"I don't think so."

"You were worried before. What changed your mind?"

"Everything we see indicates a comparatively advanced level of law and order. I think the animal savagery of their ancestors has been refined out of them."

"And you're willing to gamble your life to find out?" Bill asked.

Neal hesitated. "I certainly have no right to gamble yours."

"I'll ride along," Bill said.

Neal smiled briefly. "I hope my scientific curiosity isn't the death of us."

"We can leave any time we want to."

But then the situation suddenly changed. A frantic chattering burst upon their ears. They turned to see two small simians looking in at them—chattering, gesticulating, bouncing up and down in true chimp fashion.

A crowd quickly gathered as Neal and Bill waited, silent and alert, but entirely helpless. A representative cross-section of this world's monkey population now peered at them from all directions, from every possible vantage point both around them and overhead. The nearby trees quickly became thick with ugly, peering faces.

The chatter was deafening, but Neal, even in this tense situation, retained enough academic interest to comment, "They have a definite language. No more primitive than that of some of the undeveloped tribes in our world."

Bill was not interested. He gripped the periscope tube of the scanner as being the only thing available that even remotely resembled a weapon.

"It looks like they plan to eat us for breakfast!"

"I doubt it. They're probably noncarnivorous. Just sit still. Make no hostile motions. It's all we can do."

The simians did not move in. They peered and chattered and evidenced great excitement, but that was all.

"They're afraid of us," Neal said.

"Then why don't they run?"

"Safety of numbers. It's the same with our own people. Group courage."

"They seem to be waiting for something."

Then, what they were waiting for appeared to arrive. Three massive gorillas, led by a smaller, officious chimpanzee. This quartette was marked by a difference in clothing. All the clothing worn in this monkey world was crude and drab by advanced standards, but more care had been taken with those of the new arrivals.

"Uniforms," Neal said.

"They're policemen!"

"I think so," Neal replied.

The gorillas made no move to rush in. In fact, they were the least excited of all. They stood in a line, their arms hanging motionless from the surprisingly erect position that nature had evoluted into the simian body. Obviously, they awaited the command of the chimp chief who had swung into a tree and was assessing the situation from an overhanging branch; a more commanding position, but also, one of greater safety.

The crowd had fallen silent, awaiting the decision of the chimp that no doubt represented authority to them.

"I'm going to find out something," Neal whispered.

Bill watched as Neal took from his pocket the plastic lighter he'd brought along. He snapped it and held it out so that the flame was in plain sight.

The result was negative. Sight of the flame generated no excitement.

"They've discovered fire," he said. "It's no surprise to them."

The chimp in command was watching through bright, inquisitive eyes. He chattered at them and waited for a reply. When none came, he chattered some more. A rising inflection in his voice indicated that he was asking questions.

"No doubt he wants to know who we are and what we're doing here," Neal said.

"Why don't you tell him?"

The threat of instant death apparently set aside, Bill also found himself reacting to the comical side of the picture even though the situation was far from funny.

"I'll ask them where we can find the nearest travel bureau," Bill said.

Neal did not answer. He had taken out his pipe and was in the process of lighting it. There was an immediate stirring. It ran through the watchers like a wave. A new excitement as Neal blew a cloud of smoke out through his nostrils. Even the lethargic gorilla trio peered in amazement and grumbled at each other.

The chattering had swelled anew, but it angered the chimp chief who turned his attention to the crowd and scolded in shrill tones. The effect was immediate. Silence fell instantly.

"They don't smoke, that's obvious," Neal said. "They took fire in their stride, but smoking amazes them."

"Then don't stop. Blow them a real cloud."

"Another thing. They respect authority. That one chimp is in complete control."

"Maybe we ought to start asserting ourselves. Maybe they'd accept authority from us."

Again, Neal did not answer, and Bill noted his calm attitude—a little out of place, Bill thought, under the circumstances. Neal could have been in a laboratory back home. His expression was abstract, thoughtful, his manner totally academic.

Bill shifted his weight, preparing to rise, but Neal touched his arm. "No. Take it easy. We don't know enough about them yet."

The chimp leader suddenly made his decision. He chattered a command and the three gorilla policeman moved stolidly forward.

Again Bill started to rise, but Neal restrained him. "Hold it. Don't do anything they could interpret as hostile."

Even as the trio pushed into the bushes, Neal remained the impersonal scientist. "The pattern is right," he said. "Brains commanding brawn. The chimpanzee is the smartest simian. The gorilla is the brawn."

The gorillas were brawn indeed. Two of them lifted Neal by his arms, like a doll, and hoisted him into the clear where he stayed on his feet. The third one handled Bill all alone, looping a gray-clad arm around his middle and carrying him like a sack of meal.

Then one of the two that had brought Neal out went back for the scanner. Both Neal and Bill had qualms at this point, but the gorilla was careful with the scanner, not damaging it in any way.

Now the chimp came down from his perch and a few moments later a peculiar rig hove in sight along one of the narrow paths; a flat, four-wheeled cart, pulled by a small dinosaur-type beast.

Neal remained bemused. "A fantastic mixture of the modern and the primitive," he murmured. "Almost a caricature. But this world is only semipermanent. It can't possibly last."

Bill's mind was on less abstract matters. He watched as the gorillas loaded the scanner onto the platform and the ugly, baboon rider slapped the dino into movement.

Neal and Bill found that they were not going to be carried to their destination when the chimp chattered and motioned and the whole group moved forward with the crowd surging around them. Neal's pipe was the great center of interest. The fascinated monkeys ducked in to peer at the smoking process, then ducked back to chatter excited comments at their fellows.

As befitted a leader, the chimp chief paid no attention, walking importantly along beside Neal and Bill, but ignoring them personally.

Neal's momentary interest was on the dino. "Notice the evolutionary refinements," he said. "There is prime evidence here of Nature's first command: *Refine or perish.* These beasts have become much smaller than their ancestors. The neck of this one has lost all serpentine aspects. The creature has leveled out and stopped using its tail as a base of support. The armlike foreparts have developed into legs."

"Isn't that wrong?"

"What do you mean—wrong?" Neal asked.

"Well, I'm not quite sure myself, but it seems opposite from the way the monkeys have gone. The ones back in our zoos spend a lot of time standing on their arms, walking on them. But these are erect. They don't lean forward on their knuckles."

"I see what you mean. The monkeys appear to be going in the right evolutionary direction."

"Yes—toward a refinement. But the dinos and bronts going down on all fours looks to me to be just the opposite."

"But they've gotten off their tails."

"That's true."

"Actually," Neal said, "we've got to be ready to suspend our previous ideas. We see proof here, I think, that Nature really does as she pleases in her experiments. She is not bound by our preconceived laws."

"You said this world could only be semipermanent. How can you tell?"

"That, at least, does seem logical. If we still accept the refinement theory, and we have to, because it's all we've got, we must assume that nature is failing here and will eventually give up. She is not getting anywhere."

"Good lord! She's turned zoo animals into civilized, self-governing creatures!" Bill protested. How can you say she's failed?"

"Because other experiments she's engaged in have turned out so much better. Here, all she's achieved is an unsatisfactory compromise, a blending of old and the new. She has made infinitely greater progress with you and me and our world. So, if logic means anything at all, she will have to give up on the monkey eventually."

Bill smiled faintly. "But you said it yourself—we can't really be sure of anything until we have the final answer."

"You're getting pretty sharp, young man," Neal murmured in good-humored annoyance. "But right now, it looks as though we've arrived."

The cavalcade had stopped at one of the houses. Close to structures now, Neal and Bill could see that none of them had first floors. The pole entrances into high uncovered doorways were a common architectural factor.

The chimp leader pointed at the pole and issued a command. Neal and Bill looked at each other. "He's ordering us to climb," Bill said.

Neal's comment was milder. "Perhaps he's inviting us."

"Is there a difference?"

"We could find out by refusing."

Bill folded his arms, and while his manner was not hostile, it nevertheless was firm. It said, no.

The chimp chattered again. Bill did not move.

The next command was directed at one of the gorillas. There was a grunt of acknowledgment and the simian moved forward. He seized Bill in his beamlike arms and tossed him into the air—a dozen feet up the pole.

Bill barked a protest as he hung for a split second at the top of his ascent and then did the instinctive thing—grabbed at the pole for support on his way down.

When he arrived at the bottom, his arms around the monkey version of a stairway, he found Neal grinning. Neal said, "That clarified things a little. You climb or get thrown through the door. Which do you prefer?"

"I guess I'd better climb."

Bill set himself for the climb, then paused as Neal looked at the command chimp and motioned toward the scanner. In a sort of questioning pantomime, he inquired as to whether they could take the scanner up with them.

The chimp answered in the cryptic language of the monkeys, and then stood glaring at Neal. The latter, however, did not back down. He went firmly through the gestures a second time, and again there was an explosion from the chimp; to a point where Bill cut in.

"Watch it, Neal. You're making him mad."

"I think he's angry because we can't understand the language and because he can't understand ours. I'll risk one more try. Keeping the scanner with us is worth it."

Neal gave the chimp a placid smile and went through it again, but more slowly this time, keeping good humor uppermost. The chimp responded this time with a gesture of resignation that was comically human. Immediately, Neal laughed boisterously. The chimp responded.

"Do you remember the old saying?" Neal asked quietly. "Monkey sees, monkey does?" Then he added quickly, "But for heaven's sake, don't ever give them the idea we're ridiculing them or we're in any way contemptuous. It's all right to laugh if we laugh with them."

The gorillas, two of them, had come forward at a command from the chimp. Bill watched fearfully as they picked up the scanner. Would they merely heave it up through the opening? They were certainly strong enough.

His relief was obvious as they grasped the mechanism, each with one hand, and used the other to go up the pole with a lithe ease that the physical structure of their species alone made possible. They deposited the scanner inside and came lethargically back down to await further orders. It occurred to Bill that they would probably have killed their prisoners, if so ordered, with the same casual unconcern.

But as things stood, there seemed little cause for worry. They had the scanner with them and could leave the simian world whenever they chose.

Now the chimp chattered another command, his gestures making it completely understandable. He expected Neal and Bill to climb the pole.

Neal shrugged. "All right, do you want to go first?"

Bill, feeling ridiculous, wrapped his legs around the pole and gripped it overhead. "I feel like a fireman, except they slide down poles. They don't climb them."

The monkeys thought it was ridiculous also. The sounds that followed Bill's clumsy, struggling ascent, were obviously monkey laughter. Nor did Neal's dry comment help any: "You're making us look bad, I'm afraid."

Bill finished the climb and tumbled into the opening above. "Okay, it's your turn now. I'll bet you can't even make it."

But Bill was wrong. He stared in amazement at the ease with which Neal climbed the pole. Amused at Bill's surprise, Neal enjoyed the situation. "I went out for track in college," he said, and added with elaborate nonchalance, "Some people have a natural athletic ability."

The room was crudely furnished. There was a low, square table, but no chairs. Instead, several body-sized pads were strewn about the floor. They were covered with the same gray cloth out of which the simian's clothing was made.

"Evidently, they don't sit down," Neal said.

"I hope they eat, though," Bill retorted. "I'm hungry. Do you suppose they intend to feed us?"

A reply was not necessary because at that moment an incredibly ugly baboon appeared at the top of the pole. He, or she—they had been unable to tell the difference—carried a tray generously loaded with fruit. Timidly, the baboon set the tray on the table and lunged for the pole, obviously unwilling to remain alone in the company of these two strange creatures.

Bill examined the tray. "No bananas," he said.

The meal was made up of apples, pears, grapes, and peaches.

"Interesting," Neal said. "This menu tells us a great deal about them."

"It tells me that they like fruit. But I knew that before we got here."

"But there are no tropical or semitropical fruits. That indicates a primitive civilization in that they stay where they are, in this temperate belt. Long-distance transportation is unknown to them."

Bill restlessly paced the room. "You're right, but I can't get too interested. I don't see that it matters to us one way or the other."

"Anything we can learn is of interest," Neal said.

"But I'm more concerned with moving on. I'm pretty sure we aren't going to find Dad in this crazy world."

"I wonder if he passed this way?" Neal murmured.

"We'll ask him when we see him. Let's get into our suits and move on."

Neal pondered this. "You're probably right. There's no use pressing our luck. These creatures are probably unpredictable. It's difficult to say what they might decide to do with us tomorrow."

The suits had been rolled up and carried on top of the scanner unit. Bill unrolled them. He began donning his own and Neal reluctantly followed suit.

Experienced now, they went through the routine of taking off. The one-two-three. The tap on the shoulder.

But nothing happened. They looked at each other, then looked about them. Nothing had changed.

"Maybe it's the same as that first time," Bill said. "We haven't moved far enough to change the scene."

Frowning, Neal shook his head. "No. The scanner didn't function."

"Then they broke something carrying it over here."

Neal made a quick check—all that was necessary to discover the trouble.

"There was a small rheostat that plugged in on this side. It's gone."

"That head chimp! He must have taken it out."

Neal nodded. "They're smarter than we gave them credit for."

"Now we *are* in trouble."

"At least, we aren't going anywhere until we get it back."

"What shall we do?"

"I suggest we eat an apple—and wait," Neal said.

Ordeal by Fire

"SO THE PICTURE CHANGES," Neal said grimly. "First, I owe you an apology."

"An apology for what?" Bill asked.

"You wanted to leave before they discovered us there in the park. It turns out that would have been the smart thing to do."

Bill found himself embarrassed. "Stop it! We aren't dead yet. And if we can't out-think a few partially civilized monkeys, we don't deserve to get away."

"I appreciate your attitude. And now, maybe we'd better start thinking.

Bill's eyes had swung to the entranceway. "What do you suppose they're doing out there."

He referred to a gathering of simians in what was obviously the village square. Those that had been crowded around the prison house had joined others in the open space and it now appeared as though the entire population of the village had come together.

Neal frowned. "I don't like it."

"But they aren't threatening us. It looks like some sort of a celebration—a kind of Mardi Gras."

The simians were dancing. The chattering had taken form, had become a chant—rhythmic, with a sort of funereal beat.

They're dancing," Neal said.

"Some kind of a snake dance."

They were all in single file now, moving to a slow beat in twisting, interweaving pattern that filled the square.

"I don't like it," Neal repeated. "Especially that platform on the far side. It wasn't there before."

"You've formed some definite idea of what's going on," Bill said.

Neal answered indirectly. "I'd hoped religious instincts had not yet developed in them. But . . ."

"You think that's a religious rite?"

"It looks that way."

"But why does that worry you?"

"Primitive religious practices have one thing in

common, particularly the more barbaric ones. Sacrifice. The taking of life as propitiation to heathen gods. In many cases, animals are sacrificed. Often, however, the offerings are human."

"Good lord! Then maybe we're going to be—"

"Offered up," Neal said grimly. "That looks like a funeral pyre to me. They've learned all about fire and its uses."

"Then we've got to do something!"

"You're quite right. But exactly what—that's the problem."

"We could slide down the pole and make a run for it."

"I'm afraid we wouldn't get very far. But even if we succeeded, we would only be escaping into a larger prison. Without the scanner, we could never escape from this world."

"But it doesn't have to be that way. Maybe they see us as gods. Wouldn't that be just as logical?"

"I'd say so, but we obviously don't fit their preconceived notions of what gods are like. Their treatment of us proved that. I don't think they'd put their deities in jail."

"Then maybe we ought to start acting like gods. There's no point in sitting here waiting to be barbecued."

"They haven't seen us in our suits," Neal said.

"Then that might do it!"

In the short time he waited for Neal's reply, Bill evaluated himself. Up to this point, the unreality of the situation had predominated. It had seemed so dreamlike—as though he had been entrapped in a fantasy that would soon burst like a bubble and be finished.

But it had not been a dream. No bubble had burst and now the reality of the situation could not be denied. Was he frightened? This uncertainty; this tense excitement. Was it fear?

Perhaps he avoided the answer as Neal said, "First, we should make whatever plans we can. Our objective is getting the rheostat from that head chimp, if he still has it, and then reconnecting it to the scanner."

"That shouldn't be any problem if they decide we're gods after all."

"We can't count on that. If we merely frighten them, they may attack and kill us without waiting for a burning."

"But regardless, we've got to go down that pole. We can't just sit here."

"You stay here," Neal said. "I'll go."

"No, sir! Not a chance! We're in this thing together and we'll stay together."

Neal didn't press the demand; possibly because he knew it would be a waste of time. Bill's tone indicated that. "All right. We'll put on our suits and go out there. Our objective is to get close to the boss chimp. From there, we'll have to play it by ear."

Then, abruptly, events took an ominous turn. Even as they were getting into the suits, they realized the chanting had stopped. And as they glanced out, they saw that the monkeys had stopped the dance as well as the chanting. They were now gathered in a circle around the platform upon which the wood for the sacrificial fire had been placed, and they appeared to be awaiting the next development.

Now, Neal and Bill saw the fire; three blazing brands held by baboons dressed in robes rather than garments common to the rest. They held the torches aloft and began another ritual dance.

Then the three gorillas reappeared, coming swiftly into the room by way of the pole. They stopped at sight of Neal and Bill in the suits. To the gorillas, they seemed to have become different creatures.

But the pause was momentary. They had their orders and were capable only of carrying them out. They exhibited no fear whatever, and only the slightest confusion.

Resistance was useless. Any one of the gorillas had twice the combined strength of Neal and Bill. They were seized and carried easily down the pole, each by one of the simian police, the third merely followed along after.

A ripple of chattered interest swept the onlookers as the prisoners were brought forward. But it was subdued and it ended quickly. A spirit of religious awe prevailed, chilling in its primitive intensity.

"I see one chance," Neal said. "They have nothing to use for weapons, either. So if we get the opportunity . . ."

He got no further. The gorilla that was dragging

him along by one arm, turned, snarled, and slapped out angrily. Evidently this was a time for silence.

The blow was not heavy and it expended itself against the helmet of the suit. But even a light blow from a full-grown gorilla has force to be reckoned with, and Neal was rocked back on his heels.

He risked a further word—"follow my lead." The gorilla snarled again and raised his great arm. But when Neal fell silent, he did not repeat the punishment.

This left Bill to wonder what Neal had in mind. But even not knowing gave him some hope; and also, something upon which to fix his thoughts, thus affording him a buffer against blank fear.

As they moved through the outer circle and approached the rude altar, Bill noted with some satisfaction, that the leader, the chimp they believed had taken the rheostat, stood apart from the rest in the company of the three simian priests. Bill glanced at Neal, knowing from his look that he considered this to be a stroke of good fortune.

The gorillas led them to the waiting quartette, released their arms, and stood phlegmatically awaiting further orders.

The chimp issued a brief command and they moved back some dozen feet where they stood quietly waiting.

Now the three priests went back to their rituals, moving in a circle around Neal and Bill, holding their flames aloft and chanting. The chant was picked up by the circle of faithful around the altar, and Neal seized the opportunity to whisper through the open front of his helmet.

"The head chimp has the rheostat in his pocket. I saw it."

The chimpanzee had moved back against the altar. He stood there, not joining in the chant.

"You said you had a plan," Bill whispered back.

"The torches. Our only chance. We've got to surprise them or it won't work."

"I get it. We grab the torches—"

"And try to fight our way back to the scanner—after I get my hands on that stat." He paused. "Or maybe I should say *if* I get my hands on it."

"There are three torches."

"We'll wait. Maybe they'll come a little closer to us. If not, we'll have to take our chances. Follow my lead. I'll grab for two of them. You get your hands on the other. Then we'll make a try for the stat. When you get hold of a torch, go in on the left of the chimp. I'll take the right side and let's hope he doesn't get away from us."

Bill waited, every nerve tingling. He did not allow himself to think of what a long shot the attempt would be. It was the only chance they had. If it failed, those gorillas would soon tie them on that pile of wood and . . .

Bill refused to dwell on that aspect, riveting his attention on the slowly circling priests and wishing Neal would make his play and get it over with.

The torches were brightly ablaze at one end. They

were a good three feet long, and with no other weapon against them, would certainly command respect. Then Bill wondered fleetingly if the monkeys did have weapons they had not yet brought into the open. He fervently hoped not.

The circling and the chanting continued, but the priest came no nearer. Then it stopped. The head chimp gave an order—and Neal waited no longer.

Lunging forward without warning, he seized the closest torch, got a firm grip on it, and wrested it from the grip of the surprised priests. In almost the same movement, he swung its flaming head in the direction of his second target.

The move was not quite so successful. The baboon made an instinctive backward movement. Neal lunged a second time, bringing the flaming head close to the baboon. There was a squall of indignation and pain as the fire seared the hair on the animal's face. The torch fell from his hand. Neal swooped toward it.

Bill had hurled himself forward an instant after Neal made the initial move, and caught the third baboon completely by surprise. But his own eagerness defeated him. He got his hands on the torch, but it slipped from his grasp and fell to the ground. Angry at his own clumsiness, he dived after it. By the time he had retrieved it and thrust the baboon priest back, Neal was already moving in on the leader chimp.

"Cut him off!" Neal yelled as the chimp moved to the left side of the platform.

Bill got there just in time. The chimp whimpered in the face of the searing flame and cringed back.

The gorillas stayed where they were, no order to interfere having been given. They stared, dull interest reflecting in the eyes below the sloping foreheads. And it was this need of direction demonstrated by the gorillas, that at least momentarily saved the situation for Neal and Bill.

"The stat!" Neal cried, spreading his torches wide to hold the chimp at bay. "It's in his left-hand pocket."

Bill moved in around the flame and clawed with his free hand. "Got it!"

"Then let's go."

They were completely encircled by the startled monkeys. They had made their move so quickly, that surprise and confusion dominated. The monkeys did not attack, but neither did they move out of the way.

"We've got to cut through," Neal said. "Straight into them."

Pointing the three blazing torches ahead of them, they charged the simian wall at a point in direct line with the house in which they'd been imprisoned. The monkeys fell back from the approaching fire, squealing in anger. There were higher-pitched howls of pain from those whose retreat was blocked by rearward spectators and consequently had hair and skin singed by the torches.

But a path opened and Neal and Bill charged through. As they cleared the barrier of spectators, they heard a screeching from the head chimp, and responding growls from the gorillas.

"Okay," Neal said grimly. "Now the fight starts. The cops are coming, and they can outrun us. Our only chance is back-to-back. You keep walking straight ahead. I'm right behind you."

Their first rush had covered a third of the distance to the house, but now, as the gorillas came on, their pace was slowed to the speed at which Neal could walk backwards and defend their rear with his two torches.

The gorillas were brave. They came snarling in, with seeming contempt for the fire, until the flame bit at their hides. Each time this occurred, they somersaulted and rolled away in frenzies of snarled rage.

The spectators made no effort to interfere, remaining spectators under even these violent circumstances. Again the monkeys formed a ring—one that moved along now—keeping the action in its center.

"I hope they don't go on ahead and wreck the scanner," Neal said.

This dismal possibility frightened Bill more than anything that had yet happened and he frankly admitted to himself that he was scared.

Fortunately, he had no time to brood on the possibility, the gorillas now working in a circle, going around them in great leaps, howling rage and vengeance and seeking to break past the out-thrust torches.

Thus the situation was brought to an impasse, with Bill and Neal moving toward the pole that led up to the precious scanner.

Coming close, Neal said between thrusts of his torches, "When we get there, you've got to make the climb while I hold them off. If you reach the scanner, reconnect the rheostat and get it ready."

"But how can you make it alone?"

"There's only one way I can think of—set the house on fire. When you get there, throw those pads down to me."

The time of the real test finally came, when they stood with their backs to the wall of the house, surrounded by the entire simian population of the village.

"Throw your torch and start climbing," Neal said.

"Throw it?"

"Yes. Out there where they're packed the solidest. It may create a diversion."

Bill, one arm around the pole, obeyed, hurling his torch hard into the thickly packed simians.

This did create a diversion. There were howls of pain and distress as the frantic monkeys sought to climb and tumble and fight their way to safety.

The cause of the trapped prisoners was aided by the refusal of the untouched monkeys to fall back and give the burned ones a chance to escape. In fact, they pressed in closer to see what all the racket was about and the resulting confusion of curiosity, pain, and total panic, gave Bill the time he needed on the pole, temporarily stopping the gorillas who stood back from Neal's torches, swiveling their heads in indecision.

Glancing upward, Neal saw that Bill had made it. "Throw down the pads!" he yelled.

There were five of them and when they landed at his feet, Neal kicked them against the wall and around the pole and applied one of his torches.

The pads were dry as tinder. They caught instantly. Also, the walls of the house.

The head chimp had been blocked off by the struggles of the encircling population, but now he came raging over their heads, screaming orders at the gorillas. Only the head chimp seemed to be aware of the gravity of the situation—how close he was to losing his prisoners.

He screamed a second series of orders at the gorillas, and stirred them into action. But by this time, Neal was halfway up the pole and the pads he'd arranged as an arc of defense were throwing up a three-foot wall of flame. Also, the house was afire, yellow flames licking broadly up the dry, thin walls.

The gorillas were valiant. They made several attempts to go through the circle of fire, but the heat of the wall, its flames licking upward against Neal's laboring legs, sent them cringing back.

In the perilous room above, Bill had the scanner in readiness, and the waiting time was the longest he'd ever endured.

Then Neal's head came in view above the lower edge of the opening.

"You made it," Bill howled in triumph as he leaned forward with the end of Neal's connecting cord in his fist. "You've made it!"

"Not . . . quite." Neal grunted.

Then he rolled across the threshold and lay panting as Bill plugged him in.

The walls around them were aflame and Neal struggled to his feet. Swiftly, they went through the routine.

"One—two—three."

Neal tapped Bill's shoulder.

And now they faced it. Would the scanner work?

The ensuing moment seemed a year.

The Shining World

THEY WERE ON A BUSY STREET in a city filled with tall, clean buildings and energetic people, and no one was paying them the least attention.

"The world of tomorrow," Bill muttered.

It was as apt a four-word description as was possible, except that it didn't do the city justice. Standing there on the street, clad in the clumsy suit with the grotesque-looking scanner at his side, Neal Adams sought to expand on the description.

"Yes, but it's even more than that. It's the world of

an idealized tomorrow. One that in our own world we would dream of but could never expect."

"I see what you mean."

They stood fascinated at what ranged within their view. A girl, hurrying by, dropped an empty cigarette pack she'd taken from her bag. The package hit the sidewalk and began moving, seemingly of its own volition, and vanished into a grated opening near the curb.

"Notice the streets," Neal said. "This city keeps itself clean. Some sort of a city-wide vacuum system."

"No traffic problems, either," Bill said. He was referring to the double-level street, each level running one way with traffic moving in perfectly spaced precision.

"An electronic beam system," Neal said. "No one steers or uses brakes."

"The pedestrians look a lot safer," Bill said.

"They're riding moving belts."

"It's odd," Bill went on, "but even with this world so far ahead of ours, I still feel perfectly at home here."

"That's because it's still our world."

Bill glanced over quickly. "But I can't quite grasp that. All the worlds are in existence at the same time. How can this one be so much ahead?"

"We've also seen the ones behind. The mechanics of time are mysterious. It's almost impossible to bring its true operation within the scope of our ability to conceive. But we can be sure that all evolutionary by-paths function simultaneously. It can't be any other way."

"Confusing to say the least," Bill murmured.

"Indeed it is. But another thing seems apparent. All nature's experiments have, or rather, *are* contributing to the perfection of this world, which, I'm sure, is comparative in respect to the progress and perfection that lie ahead in the great evolutionary cycle."

"In other words, we've come onto a more successful evolutionary path. I think you said the simian world wouldn't work."

"Doesn't this one tend to prove it?"

"It sure does." And Bill fell silent, entranced with what he saw about him.

He had difficulty in defining the architecture, even to himself. The lines of the buildings were futuristic, sleek, and functional, but even more had been achieved. There was beauty here also. The cold, impersonal image of the city of the future was missing.

But he turned his attention from the city itself to the people of the city. Their clothes did not differ greatly from those in his own world, and yet they did. There seemed less bulk to the garments. All the women wore trousers, the skirt apparently having been discarded as nonfunctional. Yet, the image of femininity had been retained.

Bill was aware of this, but only vaguely. He was watching the people go by with a rather bemused expression on his face. "They're different," he said. "But I can't say just how."

"They look more relaxed."

"Surer of themselves."

"It's in their faces. They don't look so tense."

"Evidently, science had found a few cures on the inside, too," Bill said.

No one was paying any great attention to the visiting pair. They got quite a few glances from passers-by. But if a couple of characters wanted to stand on the main street in weird, ill-fitting suits with a funny-looking box between them, it appeared to be all right with the citizenry.

"What do we do now?" Bill asked.

"I don't know exactly."

"Maybe we'd better inquire."

"Of whom? About what?"

"You've got me," Bill said, "but we can't stand here all day. Somebody will push us into the vacuum cleaner system."

"I wonder where you eat in this city?"

"What do you mean?"

"Is everything mechanized? Maybe everything comes out of coin machines."

"Then I guess we'll starve. We haven't got a coin between us."

"Let's ask a good safe question and take it from there."

"What would you consider a good safe question?" Bill replied.

"How about where's the airport? That shouldn't draw any funny looks."

"Okay. Stop someone and ask."

Stopping a passer-by wasn't difficult. Neal had only

to raise his hand and an attractive young lady stopped and smiled. "Can I help you?"

"We were wondering how to get to the airport."

"It's on top of Ohio City Complex. Walk four blocks south and go up the ramp. There are elevators to take you to the two-hundred-floor level."

Bill was about to ask which way south was but the girl was looking curiously at the scanner. She said, "Why don't you get a lifter for that thing?"

"A lifter? What's a—where can we get one?"

The girl's smile broke out full now. "What world are you two from?"

Bill and Neal looked at each other in consternation, their eyes asking the same question: What have we stumbled into here, anyhow?

Neal found his tongue first. "I'm afraid we have no intelligent answer for that, miss."

The girl seemed to understand. She was still regarding the scanner. "That's a real antique you've got there. Does it work?"

The question created other questions. What did the girl think the scanner did? Grind coffee, perhaps, Bill thought as Neal said, "Oh, yes—yes, miss. It works quite well."

"Where's the directional device?"

"It's—it's on the inside," Bill offered lamely.

The girl chuckled in completely friendly fashion. "I'll bet you have no money."

"Oh, we have money, but only paper bills from—"

"I'll buy one from you if you like," the girl said eagerly. "I collect money from other worlds."

Neal took out the roll they'd brought with them and peeled off a ten-dollar bill. "We'd very much appreciate it."

She did not ask the bill's value, appearing to be aware of it herself. Her eyes lighted like those of a true collector. "Oh, no! Why, those are priceless!"

Bill shrugged. "That one's only worth ten bucks where we come from."

"There are very few of them in existence in this world. If I gave you all the money I've got with me I'd still be cheating you."

Neal shrugged. "It's no good to us if we can't buy a sandwich with it."

"You can buy a lot more than that. Here—" The girl had taken some coins from her purse. When she dropped them into Neal's hand he found them to be practically weightless. "I'll lend you a couple of dollars."

"But how can we pay you back?" Bill protested.

The girl laughed. "That won't be difficult. In the meantime the place you want is Interplane."

"What's Interplane?"

The girl was enjoying their bewilderment. "It's what you were looking for when you asked for the airport. Go in that arcade there and get a lifter for that monstrosity you're carrying. Then go down those stairs at the end of the block and take a monocar that says Science Complex on it. Interplane is in the Einstein Building. It's a sort of hotel. They'll take care of you there."

The girl's friendliness had a bright effervescent quality to it that warmed both Bill and Neal. "It's awfully good of you to bother about us," Neal said.

"That's quite all right. When you get to Interplane ask for Doc Hayes. Tell him Marion Baylor sent you. I must run now."

She started away and then turned back to call, "And don't lose that antique of yours. It's priceless, too."

The girl hurried on and Bill and Neal looked at each other, their earlier bewilderment only slightly lessened. Neither of them found anything to say until Neal smiled wryly and put the bill back into the roll. He fingered the plastic coins in his palm.

"Well, let's do like the lady said. "Let's get a lifter."

They found what they supposed was the article she'd referred to in a dispenser in the arcade. It seemed to be nothing more than a plastic handle.

"There's a button underneath it," Bill said. "Let's try it on the scanner."

Placing the flattened ends of the handle against the surface of the scanner, they found that it adhered with rocklike solidity.

"A form of magnetism that works on plastic," Bill said.

But that was only part of it. With the handle firmly attached to the upper surface, the scanner immediately became weightless. Neal lifted it two feet off the sidewalk and it waited there to be directed as he saw fit.

Neal and Bill stared at it for a few moments. Then they looked at each other. "Let's go," Neal said.

They found the monorail on the lower level of the city, using two of the plastic coins to go through a turnstile. The trip to the Einstein Building was little more than a blur of shining walls.

As they got out of the car and stood on the platform trying to orientate, Neal said dryly, "And we thought we lived in a pretty modern world."

"I see what you mean," Bill replied. "But do you see what I see up there ahead on the platform?"

Neal was already staring and together they watched what had to be a robot doing its assigned job. The robot was a box on three wheels. Its control unit constituted a head set squarely on top of the box and it had two long, flexible arms with hands that didn't match. One hand was a small box and the other was a claw, and the robot's job was to pick up refuse from the platform.

The robot had been momentarily out of work and had backed itself against the wall to await developments. As they watched, an emerging passenger threw away an empty cigarette pack. The package hit the floor some fifty feet from where the robot waited, but it went into action instantly. It rolled down the platform, grabbed the package with the claw and deposited it in the box at the end of its other arm.

"I wonder if it can cook?" Neal asked absently.

"And I'm wondering what it identifies as refuse. Not our scanner, I hope."

Evidently odd-looking mechanical contraptions the size of the scanner were not on the robot's list, because it went back against the wall and the light in its head glowed only faintly as Neal and Bill passed it.

They found an elevator and got off on the first floor of what appeared to be the Einstein Building. There they paused again to observe.

"It looks like Radio City, only—well, only more so," Bill said.

"There's a directory over there."

They found Interplane listed as being on the 190th floor and pushed their scanner toward the elevator bank. A few passengers looked at them with nothing more than casual curiosity and when the elevator had cleared, Neal commented on this.

"I don't get it. We'd draw a crowd with these suits and this scanner in any city I've ever known. Here they take us in stride."

Bill shrugged. He wasn't even trying to figure it. "Beats me," he said.

As they stepped out of the elevator, they realized Interplane whatever it was, had the entire 190th floor. There was a reception desk in front of the elevator bank and a pretty girl with a magnificent blonde hairdo smiled courteously.

"We would like to see Doctor Hayes," Neal said.

"Marion Baylor sent us," Bill added.

The girl had turned bemused eyes on the scanner. "A new invention?"

"We thought so," Neal murmured. He was mainly

preoccupied, however, in wondering why anyone as important as Doctor Hayes evidently was should bother to see them.

But when his voice came back over the intercom in response to the receptionist's call, it was cheerful and eager.

"Oh, yes. Send them right in, by all means."

Nor did this surprise the receptionist. Courtesy and friendship seemed to be the way of things at Interplane. The girl pointed to the right. "The fifth suite," she said. "You'll find the name on the door." It was as though baggily-clad strangers with outlandish equipment turned up there every day.

They found the door and went in and saw a big, smiling, white-haired man at a huge desk in the middle of a vast room. He was talking to someone on what was obviously a visiphone of some sort.

"Come over and sit down," he called. "I'm talking to a friend of yours."

They glanced at each other and moved forward after Neal pushed the scanner to the floor and snapped off the switch in the handle.

As they covered the distance between the door and the desk, Bill glanced back nervously as though he was afraid the scanner would follow them.

But it stayed where it was and when they came within the scope of the visiphone's range, another pleasant voice greeted them.

"Oh, I see you got there. Did you have any trouble finding Interplane?"

They looked into the visiphone and saw Marion Baylor sitting at a desk of her own. In the background were the obvious fixtures and trappings of a beauty shop.

"No—no trouble," Neal blurted. He'd tried to keep his voice casual and thus hide his bewilderment.

But he did a bad job of it because both Doctor Hayes and Marion Baylor laughed. The laughter was friendly, however, as Doctor Hayes said, "I think our guests are a little confused at the moment, Marion. But that's perfectly logical."

"I think you'll clear things up for them, Doc," the face in the visiphone replied.

"I'll certainly try."

"Well, I just wanted to alert you. I've got to get back to work now."

The image faded and Doctor Hayes snapped off his unit. "A wonderful girl, Marion. She ought to settle down and get married. A great waste, that girl staying single."

This comment had been made mainly to himself. Now he turned his attention on his guests. "Do sit down, gentlemen. Perhaps you're hungry. May I order you something?"

"As a matter of fact," Neal said, "we are hungry, but that's the least important of our problems at the moment."

"It's more important right now," Bill cut in, "to know where we are and—"

He stopped, unable to shape his confusion into answerable questions.

"You're in the Ohio Complex. But I doubt if that answers your question. In this world of science and progress, you'll find things a little different. Briefing you on those differences will take a little time. So why don't you get settled in your quarters first? Later, we can get together and have a nice long talk."

"You've been tremendously helpful," Bill said, "and we certainly don't want to impose. But you see, I'm looking for my father, and—"

Doctor Hayes's smile was replaced by a look of sympathetic concern. "I don't think you mentioned your names."

"I'm sorry," Bill said. "It was rude of us. Please excuse us. I'm William Franklin. My companion is Neal Adams. We—"

"And your father is—"

"Samuel Franklin." The look on Doctor Hayes's face made Bill's heart leap. "You're familiar with the name! You know my father!"

"Let's say I *knew* him. A remarkable man. A tremendous scientific brain—far ahead of the times of his world."

"Then you can tell me where I can find him."

"I'm afraid not. But please let me have you escorted to your quarters. I have some very pressing duties at the moment. I will be free in a short while and then I'll be of whatever service I'm able."

Sam Franklin Was Here

"I HAD A LONG TALK WITH YOUR FATHER, in this very room," Doctor Hayes said, "when he stopped off here."

It was a beautiful room—part of a three-room suite that looked over the Ohio Complex. "In this world," Doctor Hayes had explained, "the whole of the continent is practically one great city. The outer global surface is too precious to use in any other way. It is for the population. All food is grown artificially—underground."

So the Ohio Complex was one of many in the vastly greater complex that stretched from ocean to ocean.

Installed in the suite, Bill and Neal had been given some three hours to avail themselves of its facilities and to adjust to this new environment. Then Doctor Hayes had arrived. He'd announced that Marion Baylor would be along later. Marion, too, he'd informed them, was a most remarkable person.

But Bill had been more interested in his father and had held Doctor Hayes to that subject.

"Yes, an incredible man."

"I am just beginning to understand," Neal cut in, "how far ahead of his contemporaries, Sam Franklin was."

"The men he knew in his own aspect could hardly have been called that. He stood alone."

"Perhaps you could explain the multiple-aspect reality in clearer terms."

"Not in terms you could understand at this stage."

"But certain things are obvious. When we left our native world, we were proceeding on what was wildest theory there—a theory that a precious few of our scientists would not have laughed at."

"Quite true," Doctor Hayes murmured.

"But we arrive in a world where we're taken for granted—where travel from one world to another is an accepted thing. That's what Interplane is, isn't it? A sort of depot for interworld travelers?"

"That's a way of expressing it, but you're making a basic mistake—missing a great fundamental principle."

"What are we missing?"

"There are not *many* worlds. There is only one."

"We've begun to suspect that."

"You've seen several planes or aspects of the same world. It's a little like the blind men and the elephant. The one who grasped its tail thought it was like a rope. The one that fell against its leg thought it was like a tree, and so on. If Sam Franklin had held to the conception of myriad worlds he could not have achieved what he did. He realized he was merely moving among various planes of the same world."

"But this one is certainly vastly different from the one we just left," Neal said.

"Of course. But suppose you were in the slums of one of your cities. Would you consider it a separate city because it differed from the financial section or the industrial section or the wealthy residential section?"

"No—I suppose not."

"The reason for your illusion concerning the world is, of course, lack of perception. You are able to see so little of it at a time. Therefore the worlds you've visited appear to be separate and independent of each other."

"Sam Franklin understood this?"

"Yes. When he arrived here, he knew this was only a more scientifically advanced aspect of one world. I was greatly honored at having met him because he was able to create, with help from no one, primitive devices with which to move from aspect to aspect. That wasn't much different from the great inventor, Edison, inventing the electric light, except that Sam Franklin's task was infinitely more complex and difficult."

Doctor Hayes paused to turn his eyes toward the scanner. "That mechanism that guided your travels might be compared to using a compass to guide a rocket to the moon, except that it works. Therein lies proof of Sam Franklin's genius."

Bill had been sitting back patiently trying to contain himself while the discussion went on. Now he broke in sharply. "That's a lot of double talk! I want to find my father!"

"I understand, son," Doctor Hayes said gently.

"Please—I'm sorry if I seem unreasonable, but—"

"Please don't apologize. I realize the strain you've been under. And I wish I could be of help to you."

"You mean you can't?"

"I can't direct you to your father because I don't know where he went. As I said, he came here. He, too, sought our help and we gave him what we could. It consisted of information that allowed him to proceed more intelligently, on a less hit-or-miss basis. But that was all we could do."

"What do you mean, on a less hit-or-miss basis?" Neal asked.

Again Doctor Hayes paused to find terms that would be understandable to minds less scientifically advanced than his own.

"Let me put it this way," he said. "You are a traveler in your own native plane. You come to me in one city and inquire as to how to get to another. You are hunting for a friend of yours who might be there. I can tell you how to get to the city quite easily, but I wouldn't have the least idea whether you'll find your friend there or not."

"I'm beginning to get the idea," Neal said. "I assume from what I see around here that your advanced science allows people to move through the planes with great ease."

"Through some of them. Just as your airline systems allow people comparatively wide travel facilities. But there are places your airlines do not go. It's the same with us. We limit our movements to comparatively few planes. Just as your jets do not go where there are no landing fields, we stay away from planes where interplane travel is not facilitated."

Bill was experiencing a keen sense of frustration. Every time he tried to direct the conversation to his father, it veered off onto some other line. Still, he realized Doctor Hayes was doing his best.

"Another thing that might interest you—you were in great danger from the moment you left your native plane."

"We realized that," Neal said.

"What I mean was that you were using experimental equipment. That device you have there—and the suitlike units. They were experimental devices so far as Sam Franklin was concerned. The fact that they delivered to any destination is another tribute to his genius."

"I grant you that," Neal said, "but I don't quite

see where danger was involved as you seem to use the word. They would either have worked or left us in the shop back on our plane."

"Not at all. They could have hurled you into interplane chaos. Your lack of knowledge could have destroyed you."

This didn't seem important to Bill. They had not been hurled into interplane chaos. They had arrived in this shining world and now he was interested only in finding his father.

He was about to again call Doctor Hayes's attention to this when a bell sounded and Hayes glanced at the door.

"That will be Marion. Why don't you let her in, son."

Bill went to the door and opened it. First he saw the red hairdo, an intricate tower that he knew would have turned the teen-age girls of his plane green with envy. Then he saw the pretty girl under it and was warmed by her friendly smile.

"I came as soon as I could close my shop," she said. "I think it's terribly exciting—welcoming two strangers from a strange plane. May I come in?"

"Please do."

Marion Baylor was wearing a pair of green slacks and a white blouse. The sparkle of her personality added something to the room as she went to the chair in which Doctor Hayes was seated and kissed him on top of the head.

"It's perfectly proper," she laughed. "He's my uncle."

"Marion," Hayes explained, "is one of the more unpredictable crosses I have to bear."

"Why, that's the nicest thing I've heard all day. And now you might introduce your friends."

The introductions were made, and Bill realized why Marion had approached them in the street while others passed them by. Familiar with interplane travel, she'd been in a position to help them.

"I have an idea," Doctor Hayes said. "Marion, why don't you take the young man out and show him the sights of our complex? You two can exchange information about your planes. I've got an idea Professor Adams has a lot of his own questions he'd like to ask me."

"I think that would be wonderful," Marion said.

Bill was surprised at his own eagerness. He'd changed. It was a new thing. Back home, he would have reacted with a shyness that was now difficult for him to understand.

And that was how he landed in a fabulous rooftop restaurant by a window where a veritable fairyland of color and life lay spread out below him.

He was glad now that he'd accepted Marion's invitation. He'd never been to a place like this before, even in his own world; a place where there was candlelight and soft music and an atmosphere of luxury and romance.

And the annoyance with his old self touched him

again. Only his own earlier stupidity made him a pioneer in this area. He'd missed so much!

Marion partially sensed the trend of his thoughts. Looking at him across the snowy linen and the gleaming silver on the small table, she asked, "Is this much different from places in your plane, Bill?"

"It probably is because science reflects in every aspect of a world, and your science is more advanced than ours."

Marion laughed. "Have you got a girl friend back on your plane?"

Bill blushed and fumbled. "No . . . no, not exactly. I had friends. But I was pretty backward and . . . well clumsy, when it came to the boy-girl stuff."

"I think you're being modest, Bill."

Marion was going to add something, but Bill had been looking around at the people in the luxurious restaurant and asked, "Are there any poor people in this plane?"

"Poor? You mean without money?"

"Yes. Isn't there any poverty here?"

"Oh, no. Being without things in a world of plenty would be—well, ridiculous."

"That's certainly logical, but sometimes it doesn't work out that way."

"It does here."

But something else was bothering Bill. He frowned slightly as he continued to look around. "Doesn't anybody ever get mad?"

"Mad? Get mad at what?"

"I don't know. Just mad."

"Why should they? It wouldn't make sense. Anger is a negative emotion. It's damaging."

"Everyone here realizes that?"

"They learn it in school. A course in emotional balance is required."

Bill sighed. "I guess you've got an almost perfect world."

"No. We realize that we've only scratched the surface of scientific possibilities. We're studying and researching all the time."

"So do we, but . . ."

Marion reached out impulsively and laid her hand on his arm. "Bill, why don't you stay here? We could have wonderful times together. I'd introduce you to my friends. I know you'd like them. There's so much you've never seen that I'd like to show you."

"You make it sound awfully attractive."

He looked out across the vast complex. As far as he could see, the beauty and progress of this world was reflected like a black satin carpet spread with jewels in profusion.

He knew that cities in his own world had aspects of this sort also, but here it was different somehow; more beautiful; a subtle breadth and depth of human well-being symbolized in the glowing wonderland below.

"It looks exciting," he conceded.

Marion's characteristic laugh, like bubbles, found

a response deep inside him. How lucky could a guy get—finding all this?

"We'll talk about it further," Marion said. "But now, let's have fun. Do you dance in your plane?"

"Yes, but I'm not very good at it."

"I'll bet you're just being modest."

It was one of the most pleasant evenings Bill had ever had. It was perfect in every detail. He was forced to admit that he hadn't had many of this type to compare it with but he doubted if they would have measured up anyhow.

Back in the guest suite at Interplane, he found Neal lounging in bed with a book. He looked like a contented man.

"Well, Romeo, how was your evening?"

"Great. Marion is a lot of fun. How was yours?"

Neal considered the question before answering, and Bill realized that the tensions and anxieties of their trip through the worlds had fallen away; that he was himself again.

"Well," Neal said, "Doc Hayes isn't exactly a lot of fun, but I couldn't have had a more satisfactory evening. I learned a great deal. Bill, there are more things in heaven and earth—"

"—Horatio, than were ever dreamed of in your philosophies," Bill laughed. "I've read Shakespeare too."

"One thing—we still can't go back."

This was surprising to Bill. "I thought we were wrong, believing that when we came here. I thought it was through lack of technical knowledge. When Doctor Hayes began talking about moving from plane to plane . . ."

"I did too, but he told me something about sectors. These are divisions that contain various numbers of planes. They can move back and forth only in their own sector. It has to do with the probability-quotient of the planes, and it's so complicated it would take him several days to give me even the barest fundamentals."

"Well," Bill said philosophically, "we haven't lost anything because we didn't expect to go back in the first place."

Neal did not appear to hear. His eyes had gone vague. "There's so much to learn here, and I've had a fantastic stroke of good fortune. I've been put in a position to literally feast on the knowledge gleaned by other men through thousands of years. It's—it's breathtaking!"

"It's really a break."

"We'll stay here and sop up knowledge like a couple of sponges. Then, when we're absolutely sure of ourselves, when we've learned all that these fine people are eager to teach us, we'll go on toward our original objective."

"Doctor Hayes said he couldn't tell us where Dad is."

"That's true. We'll still have to take our chances

on that score. But with greater know-how, with the aid of their vastly improved technical equipment, we'll be in a position to proceed far more intelligently."

"That's true," Bill admitted.

Neal yawned. "I'm beat. It's been the biggest day of my life. I think I'll knock off and get some sleep." He looked at Bill and the excitement showed through his inherently calm exterior. "Maybe tomorrow will be a bigger one."

"That's possible. But I'm not sleepy yet. I'll be in a little later."

"Turn out the light, will you?"

Bill went out into the living room and sat down in front of a window where he could look out across the glowing complex. Alone for the first time in a while, he was grateful for the chance to organize his thoughts.

This wasn't the easiest thing he'd ever done. There was so much to consider, to think about; such a great deal of new knowledge and experience to assimilate. And as he sat there alone in the silence, he had to admit to himself that it wasn't assimilating very well.

He sat for a long time.

Then he got up and went to the writing desk and took out a sheet of paper and began to write:

Dear Neal:

I am very happy for you because I think you have found your world or rather, your plane. This is where you belong and where you will be happy. And I think, in exchange for what these people give you, you can give them something in return, because with your mind and dedication you will be able to.

So now I'm going on alone to find my world—the one Dad is in. I appreciate what you said about more knowledge and I realize you're right. But I haven't got time. I've got to keep on gambling. I'm sure you will understand.

I guess that's about it, so goodbye and good luck. And thanks for all you've done for me.

Bill

He read what he had written and decided it wasn't much of a letter. It didn't half express what was in his mind and in his heart.

But it was the best he could do, so he folded it and put Neal's name on it and left it on the desk.

Then he went across the room and got one of the suits out of the closet and pulled it on. He looked at himself in the mirror and realized why Marion had been amused. Living for even a day in this smooth, advanced world made him realize what an antique he was wearing.

He plugged himself into the scanner and examined the controls; one small switch; a single, fragile rheostat. He looked around the safe, comfortable room.

And he realized how scared he was. He and Neal had had a lot of luck. Doctor Hayes, who knew his business, had said this equipment was dangerous. What if their luck had run out?

But he was even more scared of those words *safe*

and *comfortable*. If he allowed them to, they could change everything.

He could not allow them to do that.

He took a deep breath. Then he pressed the switch and threw the stat forward to its limit.

The Day the God Came

A FRIGID WIND HIT BILL FULL IN THE face. He turned away from it instinctively and saw moving figures on his left. But he saw them only fleetingly because his eyes teared from the wind. He closed them and felt ice forming on his lashes.

He was on a small hillock with a boulder-dotted plain stretching in all directions as far as he could see through narrowed, streaming eyes. An arid, barren, cheerless place under a heavy sky. And bitter, bitter cold.

The wind was a steady, whining blast. Laden with fine snow, it set a hallmark of hostility on this empty land.

A man could die here.

Bill, acting possibly from habit, had disconnected his suit from the scanner and taken a few steps away from the wind. Then he realized there was no point in staying where he was. He turned back and reached for the cord that was whipping like a snake in the wind. He got his hands on it and twisted around and reinserted the plug into his suit with fingers already so cold he had lost the sense of touch.

The switch had released automatically and the rheostat had returned to zero as they always did upon arrival. He found the switch only by identifying the lump at his belt and somehow got the fingers of his other hand around the rheostat handle.

But it was too late. The button was rigid. The rheostat handle refused to work. In the brief time since his arrival, they both had frozen.

Quick panic hit Bill. Was this to be the end?

Then quick anger took over. It wasn't fair! In fact, it was degrading after what he and Neal had gone through, to come now to this frigid wasteland and turn into a frozen corpse before he could even get his bearings. It was a disgrace and he wouldn't permit it. So it was cold. So what?

But breathing defiance and icicles at the same time was difficult. Turning his back to the blast, Bill began flailing his arms against his sides and jumping up and down. He wished his father had had the foresight to put a fur lining in the suit, but it was too late for that.

The flailing and the jumping got some results in that his fingers began hurting like fury and every time his feet hit the ground they seemed to land on a bed of spikes. But at least he was showing some resistance to the cold.

Having assured himself that he could fight the cold for at least a reasonable time, he turned his attention to the scanner. It had to be gotten into some kind of shelter. There were delicate parts inside that would be vulnerable to the fine driving snow if not the cold itself.

There was a pile of rock over to the left that gave faint promise and he ran to it and found that there was room for the scanner in a pocketlike shelter on the lee side. Not total protection, but better than none.

He returned and lugged the scanner back to the rock pile and did what he could for its protection. He thought of crawling in after it and trying to thaw out his suit with his own body warmth. But it didn't seem that he had enough of that to spare. Maybe this icy purgatory wasn't as deserted as it appeared to be. He would never know unless he looked.

So he reserved his retreat into the cave as a last stand and squinted out across the jagged terrain. Again he saw the moving figures. He'd paid little attention at first, but now he studied them and decided they were either animal or human. They were merely small blots of black movement from where he was, several grouped together with a single one on ahead. As he watched, the group seemed to be chasing the single blot. Was it a hostile action? Bill thought it probably was because hostility was so much in keeping with this devil's playground.

They were paying him no attention, but this was logical because of the light gray color of Bill's suit. It blended perfectly into the haze created by the fine, driving snow.

Without further thought on the subject, Bill ran in the direction of the figures. Perhaps this was suicidal, but no more so than standing there wondering whether it was or not, so he made no effort to be clever about it. He simply ran in that direction.

The cavalcade was crossing in front of him from right to left so he ran at a leftward tangent, his feet stabbed with agony each time they touched the steel-hard ground.

He saw that the group was gaining on the single figure and, as he came closer, the sound of his foot-steps covered by the steady keening of the wind, he approached close enough to hear the cries of rage, cries that now came faintly against the wind but could still be defined for what they were.

He could make out the figures now. They were hu-man; men swathed in clumsy furs that made their going slow, thus giving Bill a chance to catch up.

The single figure in front was losing ground. Obviously, the man realized this. He glanced back over his shoulder. Then, as Bill stumbled over a small rock and fell flat, the man turned and pulled the cord of a short, stubby bow and sent a shaft back at his pursuers.

He was either a master with the weapon or he was lucky, because, as Bill came up on his hands, one of the rearward group screamed and flung up his arms to claw at his chest.

Made bold by his hit, the victim of the chase snatched another shaft from the quiver on his shoulder and fitted it to the bow. He drew back the cord and the pursuers dropped to a man and hugged the ground as the shaft rocketed over them.

Now the victim had decided to hold his ground. He brought out a third shaft. But the zest for pursuit had soured and the group had picked up their fallen member and were making a clumsy retreat. Realizing this, the bowman held his shaft. Remaining alert with the bow half drawn, he waited to see if the retreat would continue. It did. With cries of anger and promised vengeance, the group bore their wounded back as they'd come, the man's screams of agony growing faint upon the wind.

Bill came to his feet; he wondered what to do— follow the defeated ones in search of aid or attempt to approach the victorious bowman. If he decided on the latter, the third shaft might easily be his reward. But the group was now almost out of sight.

Then fate took a hand. As Bill was about to follow those who had retreated, the lone bowman swayed, dropped his bow, and fell to the ground.

Drawing his legs up, he lay in a huddled heap. Bill

ran in his direction. He was upon the man before the latter became aware of his presence. The fallen man froze for a moment, then lunged toward his bow.

Bill put his foot on it as he went to one knee. "It's all right!" he cried. "I'm not going to hurt you. What happened? I didn't see them fire anything at you."

The man's face wreathed in a fur parka was brown and leathery and twisted in pain. "My leg gave away. It's broken. I had to stop and fight."

"You ran all that way on a broken leg?"

"You do what you have to as long as you can. Who are you? Where did you come from?"

"That doesn't matter now. Where are *you* from? How far is it to your village?"

"My village?"

"Look! I'm freezing to death and you ask foolish questions. Don't you know what a village is?"

"Isn't that thing you're wearing warm enough?"

"Does it look warm enough? I might as well be standing here in my underwear."

"Then you'd better follow them and get the fur off the man I killed."

"What do you mean? He wasn't dead."

"He is by now. When I loose a shaft I know where it goes. Follow them. They'll leave him. They won't carry a dead man."

None of it made any sense but neither did standing there freezing to death. So Bill turned and ran in the direction the group had taken.

Five minutes later he came upon the fallen man and

the prophecy of the broken-legged bowman proved true. Even a superficial examination told Bill the man had indeed fallen victim to deadly marksmanship.

The instinct for survival predominating all else, Bill stripped off the loose, outer fur garment the man had worn. He tried not to look at the fast-stiffening figure on the ground and he got into the life-saving fur. He pulled the parka up over his head and could not feel its contact with his flesh. But as he trotted back toward the place the bowman had fallen he was pretty sure his ears would soon come alive with the special agony of warmth returning to numbed members.

The man had retrieved his bow and had a shaft fitted into it but his defiance was a pose he could probably not have backed up; not from the look of pain and exhaustion on his face.

"Thanks for helping me out," Bill said. "Now let's see what we can do for you."

"Not much. I'm too far from home. They wouldn't have seen me if I hadn't got careless and smashed my leg."

From the tone of the man's voice Bill got the idea that he felt he deserved what had befallen him. Evidently getting careless was the unforgivable sin of this bleak land.

"How far is your home?"

"Five marches north. I came down for salt. The salt flats are in their country and they try to kill anybody who comes after it."

It didn't seem important to Bill who *they* were or why risking death to get salt was worthwhile; not at the moment at least.

"Have you got a base or a camp somewhere around here?"

"I was holing up in a cave near the salt flats."

"How far is that?"

"Too far to go on a broken leg."

"Let's have a look. Which leg is it?"

The man put his hand on the crippled member and his look of pain increased.

Bill sought to feel through the fur but the man pulled away. "I think it was only cracked till I ran on it."

"We'll try to get back to your cave. Get up and put your arm over my shoulder and we'll walk on three legs."

The man seemed quite pessimistic about the results, but he did not object. Bill helped him to his feet and they began pressing slowly forward.

They moved in silence, the man's painful effort too great to carry on a conversation. They threaded among the rocks, seeking to find the smoothest going, and as time passed Bill began to think the man had been right. It was too far for a broken-legged man, even with help.

But then, as the darkened skies began getting even darker—signaling the fact that somewhere the sun was going down, the man gasped. "There it is. That pile right there."

It was a deceptive heap of stone in that it looked to be too small to hide the mouth of a cave. But the man directed the removal of two of the larger rocks and the opening was apparent.

Bill helped the man down the incline and followed him to find a sizable cave, faintly lit by the remains of a fire.

"There's fuel in that corner," the man said, and Bill looked and found dried spindlings from the bushes that he'd seen huddled here and there on the surface. Also, there were heavier dried branches broken into serviceable length.

He soon had a fire going and was happy to find that it did not fill the cave with smoke. A natural draft sweeping in through the chinks between the rocks moved the smoke upward and away.

For the first time since Bill had known him, the man smiled. "I didn't think we'd make it."

"We were lucky, but now you'll have to tell me what to do—after I fix up your leg, that is. Back home, I was a Boy Scout. I took the first aid course."

The man looked bewildered. "What's a Boy Scout?"

"All good guys have been Boy Scouts at one time or another," Bill said cryptically. "It's warm enough to get out of your furs now, so we'll see what we can do."

The man was short and stocky, as had been his pursuers, and Bill decided that was probably a physical characteristic of the people on this plane. The leg had not swollen as much as seemed justified for the abuse it had taken and also, from what he could tell, the break was quite clean, the bone not having been ground up. The man had tools and Bill fashioned some flat splints from the thicker branches of firewood and applied the splint, tying it with leather thongs from the man's big packsack.

The man maintained stoic silence during the whole time Bill worked on his leg. When the operation was finished the man's sigh indicated the foritiude he'd displayed.

"I think it will be all right," Bill said. "I'm no surgeon, but I think its not swelling as it might have shows it will knit quickly."

"I've got some dried walrus there in that pack if you're hungry."

"How about you?"

"I could eat."

Bill got the stringy, unappetizing-looking meat from the pack. "How do I prepare it?"

"Prepare it? You just eat it."

The man took a length of the stuff and began working on one end with his teeth. Gradually, it disappeared into his mouth.

Bill followed his example. It was like trying to draw nourishment out of the fray end of a rope. But gradually it softened up and tasted like meat.

They gnawed in silence for a while. Then the man wiped his mouth with the back of his hand and asked, "Are you a god?"

Bill blinked. The rhythm of his chewing broke and

he took the meat out of his mouth. "I beg your pardon?"

"I asked if you're a god?"

"I don't think so. In fact I'm quite sure of it. No, I'm not a god."

"Then who are you?"

"My name is William Franklin. What's yours?"

"Gallow. I'm from the lake country. That's up north."

"What country is this?"

"The middle country."

"This is where they have the salt."

"That's right."

"You came to steal—pardon me, I mean get the amount of salt you could carry away on your back."

"That's right."

"But that isn't very much salt."

"It's enough to make me rich."

"The people here in the middle country—wouldn't they sell it to you?"

"Why would they do that? It's their salt. They want to keep it."

"They'd have killed you if they'd been able."

Gallow shrugged. "Why not? If they came to the north country, we'd kill them."

"Why?"

"Why? You ask foolish questions."

"Then this is a world where everybody kills everybody else?"

"What do you mean *a* world? What other world is there?"

Bill realized now what a luxury it had been to be in the world of science where explanations were unnecessary. How could he explain the truth to this man? How could you explain addition to a man who had never heard of numbers?

"Is it warmer south of here?"

"Warmer? No. Why should it be?"

"The closer you get to the equator—"

"What's the equator?"

"A line running around the middle of the earth."

"What do you mean, the middle?"

"The earth is round, you know."

Gallow stared incredulously. He obviously thought Bill was mentally unbalanced. "That's silly. The earth is flat. It's not round out there. Any fool can see that."

"How far south have you ever been?"

"I'm a traveler. I go many places. I went deep into the south country looking for things I could take back to the north country to sell."

"And it was just as cold as it is here?"

"Colder, when the wind blows harder."

Another world where solar possibility had dictated destiny? A world where an aging sun had doomed its planets to frigid extinction?

It certainly appeared that way and Bill could only admire the tenacity of the population. They lived and carried on and accepted as their lot a frozen globe where only the hardiest could survive.

"If the people around here find you, I suppose they'd kill you?"

"They're out hunting right now."

"They don't seem very courageous. You fought off a whole group."

"Courageous?"

"I mean they seem to be cowards."

"Why? They found out I'm a good bowman. Why should they stay and get killed?"

"Well, the important thing is where you stand now. You're in hostile country with a broken leg. How are you going to get back north?"

"I'll stay in here until my leg heals. Then I'll get my salt and go home."

"There's nothing wrong with your courage."

"You didn't tell me what you were doing out there without any furs."

Bill evaded the question by asking another. "Why did you help me? Why didn't you kill me, too?"

"You can't kill a god."

"What is this god business? I don't understand."

"You're white. You had the white robe on."

"So I'm white. What's that got to do with it?"

"Everybody knows about the god of the middle country. Not long ago—"

But before Gallow could finish, there was the sound of grating rock, triumphant shouts of men outside, and the stones that formed one side of the cave were lifted away and fiercely happy, hostile faces peered down at the two trapped men.

The Perils of Godhood

BILL REALIZED LATER THAT A THING
of chance saved his life. It had grown too warm for
the furs with the fire going, so he'd removed them, but
had left the traveling suit on.

The middle country men, straining to get into the
cave, saw Gallow first. Savage and triumphant, they
jammed themselves into the cave.

Then they caught sight of Bill, who had come
partially to his feet and moved back to the far wall.

They froze and for a long moment there was no

action in the cave; until, to a man, they dropped to their knees.

The ones pressing in from the outside, eager for their share of the prey, were pushing forward but a single word went back to them.

"The god!"

Bill crouched where he was, trying to make his mind work. What was going on here? A god? What sort of nonsense? He remembered Gallow's earlier question and the references Bill had brushed aside.

The whole invading force had come to a standstill now, those inside kneeling uneasily and the ones beyond the opening peering silently in.

Bill thought fast. He had to take advantage of the mistake under which they labored. How best could he press it?

The traveling suit was of course the key, but there had to be something more than that and the fact that he was taller than they and had a white skin. His instincts told him this was a breed of men who did not bestow godhood lightly.

Then the only logical answer came so forcibly that Bill's reaction was deeply emotional.

His father had been there!

Not only that, but he had arrived among them in such a way as to have appeared to them out of nowhere. That would have been enough. A tall, white-skinned stranger materializing out of thin air.

Bill's mind raced. Was his father still there? Would

their reunion take place in a village in this bleak and hopeless world?

Bill's way was clear now. He had to assert his authority as a god. "What are you doing here?" he demanded. "Why have you come?"

The least fearful of them assumed leadership. "We came after him. He stole salt. He is from the north country."

"He is not to be harmed."

Bill realized that command would make or break him as a god. If they fell on Gallow and destroyed him regardless, Bill's newly endowed "divinity" would be of dubious value. There was nothing to do but follow ,through.

"Outside," he commanded angrily. "We'll take this man to your village."

Their hatred of Gallow was obvious as they backed out of the cave, but there was no sign of rebellion. As the cave cleared, Bill pondered the wisdom of putting the furs back on. Would they interpret that as the act of a mortal man and change their opinion of him? Better to risk that, he decided, than freeze to death before their eyes. Opinion wouldn't make much difference in that case.

Also, he drew assurance from the fact that Gallow had considered him a god, but still advised him to put on the furs.

As he picked up the garment, he said, "This man is hurt. You must carry him." When they hesitated, he pointed to the man who had had the courage to answer his first question.

"You—appoint four of your men to carry him and we will go to your village."

They obeyed him in silence although he could see that the four chosen ones would much rather have buried their knives in Gallow's heart.

It was a silent cavalcade that moved off through the screaming wind across the savage, pitiless plain. Did the wind ever stop? Bill wondered. Did it eternally blow the fine, cutting sleet across this waste?

But the question came only in passing. His mind was upon his father and what had happened to him. Would he be in the village when they arrived?

Bill was disappointed. Sam Franklin was not there. The realization was a tremendous letdown, and Bill wondered if it had been mere wishful thinking on his part. Perhaps Dad had not been there in the first place.

The village consisted of thirty or forty crude huts of rock and frozen mud and it occurred to Bill that only the environment made them different from the village in the simian world from which he had been lucky to escape with his life. Would he be as lucky here?

It occurred to him also that he had found a norm —an unchanging aspect of all the worlds—the human animal himself. Wherever he was set down, his instinct for a home and a gathering place with his kind persisted. The villages in the world of icy desolation. The

sky-tall luxury buildings of the shining world he had
just left.

But now his mind was turned to things of the moment, because the people of the village had come out
to greet the new arrivals and their awe and wonder
were apparent.

The man Bill had designated as leader was shunted
aside by another, an older man who filled the role with
more authority. His attitude toward Bill was the same,
however; he was the soul of deference as he bowed
and said, "The house where the other stayed is waiting.
No one has lived in it since he left."

There had been another! But whom? His father or
some other adventurer along the trail between the
worlds?

"We'll go there," Bill said, trying to frown like a
god. "And we do not want to be disturbed."

They did not question his decision as they led him
to a hut that was somewhat larger than the rest. Outside there stood a raised platform that indicated some
sort of ceremony might have taken place.

Bill directed that Gallow be carried inside. Then,
asserting his prerogative as a god, he closed the door
in the faces of his worshipers.

Gallow had been put in one corner of the single
room on a pile of furs. A brisk fire warmed the place
and, beside what Bill had seen in this world's accom-
modations, this was almost luxurious.

There was a knock on the door and Bill opened it.

No one entered, however, and he stepped outside to find a befurred girl kneeling with a tray of generously piled food.

But he was more interested in the rest of the scene; a circle of men around the door with spears pointed in his direction.

He scowled imperiously and the effect was strange, to say the least. They dropped to their knees and bowed their heads in total submission.

But they didn't lower the spears that encircled him in a ring of razor-sharp death.

He motioned briskly, still scowling, and the girl got to her feet and carried the tray inside. When she came out again she genuflected, her eyes wide with awe, and then scurried through the ring of spears and was gone.

Bill failed to understand the contrast of worshipers who threatened him with violence. He did not know what to do so, following what seemed to be the wisest course, he did nothing. Scowling even harder, he turned in what he hoped was an appearance of complete fearlessness and went back into the hut.

It was the first time he and Gallow had been alone since the invasion of their cave and Bill was curious as to what his attitude would be. Gallow lay silent, his eyes on Bill. They didn't mirror the awed deference in those of the villagers, but there was a guarded respect and possibly some fear. Bill hoped his new status wouldn't silence the man. He carried the tray from the table upon which the girl had placed it and put it on the floor beside Gallow's pile of furs. Then he himself sat down cross-legged and picked up a piece of the meat.

"They're not going to let you go this time," Gallow said.

"This time? What happened last time?"

"The other god left."

"Did you see him?"

"No. The way the story is told, he appeared out of nowhere—just appeared to a big party of hunters from this village."

"Did he have anything with him?"

"Some kind of a thing to ride in, I guess—from what was said. Or maybe it wasn't; tales get twisted in the telling."

"What did they do?"

"They brought him and the thing he had with him here—right into this hut, I guess. Then they came one morning and he was gone."

"I guess they didn't like losing their god."

"That's why they've got a guard out there. They're going to see that you stay."

"But I've got a—a *thing* with me too. It's hidden in a cave near the place I found you. I've got to have it."

"Why don't you get it, then?"

Gallow's tone implied that should be no problem for such as Bill.

There was another interruption; another knock on the door. This time, however, the visitor entered. It was the patriarch of the village, the elderly one who had taken charge upon Bill's arrival.

He dropped to his knees and pointed to Gallow. "What are we to do with him?"

"What would you like to do with him?"

The man was quite frank. "We'd like to kill him," he said.

"Why?"

"Because he is an enemy."

"But he is my friend."

This seemed to suffice. The man put his forehead to the ground and then got to his feet.

"He is my friend," Bill repeated, "and I do not want him harmed. He has a broken leg. When it gets well, I want you to give him all the salt he can carry and send him home."

The oldster was shocked at this order. He glared at Gallow venemously and Bill wondered if he had strained his new authority. Maybe these people might decide that kindness to an enemy was too great a price to pay for the luxury of having a god in town.

The patriarch left without comment and Bill thought he might be leaving to think it over.

But Gallow seemed confident. "You've saved my life " he said. "They wouldn't dare kill me now." There was wonder in his expression. "This is the strangest thing that ever happened to me. I will tell my children and their children and it will become a story to be told again and again. It will make me a great man."

Bill, his spirits dropping dangerously, wondered about that. Maybe this stupid world wouldn't last that long. Before Gallow's children's children heard about Bill Franklin, it might congeal completely and quit turning on its axis.

"I've got to get my machine," Bill said. "I've got to make them let me bring it here."

"I can get it for you."

"That's ridiculous. If they won't let me out—"

"They don't care about me. I think they'd like it if I wandered into the wind and died."

"You mean they'll let you come and go as you please?"

"Why not?"

"It's still out of the question. You've got a broken leg and you don't know where the machine is."

"I can find it if it's in a cave where you said. And I can use a stick to walk with."

"It's very heavy."

"I'm strong."

"Well, we can't do anything until tomorrow. Let's get some sleep now."

The hut was feebly lit by rag wicks burning in pans of oil. The windows were covered by skins tanned thin enough for movement of form to be seen on the outside. Bill debated putting the rag lamps out, but decided the illumination would make little difference, the fire actually throwing more light. He was weary and didn't anticipate any difficulty sleeping, whether the place was dark or not.

He threw himself on the pile of skins that had been provided and closed his eyes. But he'd hardly settled down before he saw flaring lights pass the window, a procession of them. He listened. The wind had died somewhat with the setting of the sun and he could hear the shuffling of many feet on the dark ground outside.

Then an unearthly wailing arose, a chorus of many voices. It grated on his ears at first, but as he listened it took on a softer, sad quality. It was a wordless dirge and there was a formless beauty in it.

"What are they doing?" he asked Gallow.

"They're asking you to help them."

"Are they short of food?"

"No."

"Are they in some kind of trouble?"

"No."

"Then why are they asking for help?"

"You're a god. A god is supposed to help. That's what a god is for."

"But they don't know what they need."

"If they knew, they wouldn't have to ask. They could get it themselves."

Bill had no answer for that and, as the dirge continued, he drifted off to sleep.

Invasion

WHEN BILL AWOKE, there was a fresh tray of food on the table. He sat up and rubbed his eyes.

Gallow was awake and already busy. "The girl brought food," he said. "I was waiting for you and I'm glad you woke up. I'm hungry."

"Go ahead without me," Bill said. "I'm not hungry."

Gallow sat on his pile of furs whittling on a long stick. "I asked them for some wood and they gave it to me."

"I slept through all that?"

"You were pretty tired."

Bill got the idea Gallow thought that rather peculiar for a god, but the north country man didn't comment further.

"What are you doing?"

"I'm making a stick to walk on. I'll put this cross-piece on top and it will go under my arm. Then I'll go and get what you want."

"If you're bound to try, take some leather thongs to make a handle."

Gallow had stopped working and was having his breakfast. Bill went to the door and looked out. The wind had picked up again and was blowing the fine, biting sleet across the empty prairie. The circle of guards stood with their spears thrust forward. They were like furry statues and for all the movement Bill saw they could have been asleep.

He closed the door. "Doesn't it ever stop snowing here?"

"For a little while in the summer. But it snows the rest of the time."

"Summer must be something."

"For a little while in summer the clouds go away. You can see the sun."

"I suppose it's nice to check once a year to make sure you still have one."

"The weather here is pretty good. It's worse up in the north country. There we have thick snow and real winds."

It seemed a sorry thing to be proud of, Bill thought, and then he was ashamed of himself. With all this whining, he certainly didn't sound like a god.

A few hours later Gallow fitted the crutch under his arm and announced that he was ready to go.

"You'll never make it!" Bill protested.

"I'll make it."

Bill told him to the best of his ability where the scanner could be found and he went out the door, hobbling along quite ably on the crutch and his broken leg.

He moved straight toward the spearmen and Bill waited for violence. But they did not even move as he passed through their ranks.

Bill closed the door and sat down on his pile of furs. His spirits were indeed low. He had no great faith in Gallow's ability to find the scanner, much less lug it back to the village on a broken leg. Somehow, he would have to sneak past the guards and reach the scanner himself. Perhaps the midnight chorus outside would not be repeated every night.

Another point occurred to him. He would have to make his move before too long. If the villagers found their prayers for help unanswered, they might let their spearmen cut him into sections to see what a false god was made of.

He threw himself down on his fur pile and wondered if they would actually run him through if he sought to break the circle. He got the idea they would and then fell to wondering about the psychology of things.

If they thought him a god, wouldn't it follow that they would not expect spears to hold him? Or even kill him?

Pondering the contradiction involved, Bill got up suddenly from where he was lying and went out the door. Not a single spearman had moved. Bill stared at them for a while and then moved slowly forward.

An inch from the line of spears he stopped. Nothing moved. He pressed forward that inch. The needle points of two of the spears went through his suit and touched his skin. He stood there for a moment and then stepped back.

One thing had become clear. They would not kill him but they were not averse to his killing himself if he chose to try going through the line.

He turned away and walked slowly back toward the door, resolved to call in the patriarch and have a showdown. This nonsense had gone far enough.

But the situation changed suddenly and banished all such thoughts. There was a shout from nearby in the village street. Bill turned and saw a man pointing. The circle of spearmen whirled also, seeing the new menace at the same time—forty or fifty armed men moving silently toward the village, the blinding sleet almost hiding them.

But they came into view now and even before the new situation dawned on Bill, he was in the midst of a pitched battle.

The assault force broke through and the defenders fought desperately to recoup. Two of them went down with spears driven through them. Almost immediately the fighting became a hand-to-hand affair and the spears were discarded for short, gleaming knives.

This isn't my war, Bill thought, and he should have retired to safety; but he stood bemused instead of retiring to the safety of his hut. Somehow, it all seemed a dream; this bitter world; the strange, hardy people who inhabited it; the unrelieved gloom and cruelty of this way of life.

But the death inflicted around him was surprisingly real for a dream, the blood that flowed and froze far more of a nightmare component.

Then Bill's bemusement was shattered as four of the invaders fought free and rushed at him. He tried to turn and escape but it was too late. They seized him and even though he fought with instinctive desperation, he was helpless against the strength of four hardy warriors.

Immediately, the battle took on new form. His capture had been observed by the rest of the assault force and a shout of triumph went up. This appeared to be a signal because the others quickly formed a savage V around Bill and his captors and set up a rearguard action as the whole force began to retreat.

The village warriors did not lack in courage. They charged viciously into the limbs of the V in attempts to rescue him. But the others were better fighters, or at least were under more skilled generalship, and before Bill knew it he was out of the village with only remnants of the defenders making attempts at rescue. Soon these too gave it up and walked or limped or crawled back toward the village.

Suddenly, Bill realized a danger he had overlooked in the excitement—that of freezing to death. He'd emerged from the hut without his furs on. In fact, he was fortunate to be wearing the bulky traveling suit, having left that on for warmth because even the interior of the hut had not been the snuggest place in the world.

So he was facing the elements in what was a losing battle.

It wasn't too hard to figure out what had happened. These new warriors, whoever they were, had invaded the village with the idea of capturing themselves a god. And they had succeeded.

What a way to treat divinity, Bill inwardly moaned as his teeth chattered and his hands and feet began to congeal. His peril was obvious and possibly imminent. Maybe this gang had different ideas of what constituted a god. They might consider him to be impervious to wind and weather. Maybe, after he froze stiff, they'd consider it only a manifestation of his power and sit around waiting for him to rise from the dead.

But this did not appear to be the case. The leader, a stocky, leather-faced man who had so ably directed the battle, approached Bill and observed him closely. After a few moments he motioned to one of his men.

The man approached. The general motioned peremptorily.

"Give me your furs."

The soldier did not hesitate. He stripped off his outer covering and handed it to the general. Underneath, there was a single garment that resembled a suit of long underwear. Stripped in this fashion, the warrior immediately turned from the squad and went running swiftly off across the open country.

This, too, was easily understood. The warrior was going home and, while it seemed impossible that he would be able to travel any distance through this subzero weather in his underwear, Bill felt it wrong to discount the abilities of these superbly conditioned people.

"Put these on," the leader suggested. There was a hilarious mixture of awe, wonder, and command in his voice, but Bill was not responding to the hilarious. He was trying to keep from freezing to death.

And nothing in his life had ever felt so good as the fur suit into which he climbed.

And now a strange rite capped the climax. After hauling Bill along like a sack of flour, after manhandling and kidnaping him, they formed a circle around him, went to their knees, and touched their foreheads to the ground.

This ceremony completed, the triumphant army got to its feet and moved on and Bill pondered the drawbacks of being a god to this motley race. It didn't get you a thing except a lot of grief.

The march was a long one from Bill's standards, but he was helped by a stubbornness that arose within him. If one of the natives could make the trip practically naked, he could handle it in a comfortable fur suit.

Several hours later they arrived at his new home, a somewhat larger village than the one from which he had been kidnaped. This one, he felt, would probably house a thousand souls.

The procedure upon arrival, however, did not vary. He was shown to a hut with a fur bed and a crackling fire and a few minutes later a girl came in carrying a tray of food.

This was welcome. Bill was hungry from the long cold hike, and it was a source of satisfaction to him that at least they fed their gods.

A little while later he discovered a variation in the pattern—the guard system. Here they did not form the semicircle around his door. Instead, the guards—a half-dozen or so—were grouped about with less discipline. However, the results were the same from the standpoint of efficiency. Bill didn't think he'd be going anywhere.

He stripped off his furs and ate almost everything on the tray and then stared into the fire for a while. Then he got up and went to the door and motioned to one of the guards.

"Come here."

The man approached and, while the others watched, he dropped to his knees and stared at the ground.

"I want to see the head man."

The guard raised his eyes. "The head man?"

"The boss, the chief, the *Führer,* the big wheel, the man in the saddle!"

The guard got up and went away. Bill went back inside and, after a while, the door opened and a man entered. Bill had expected to see the general who had engineered his kidnaping, but the man was very old. He had a withered, deeply-lined face, but there was no sign of decrepitude in the stocky figure.

Bill wasted no time in preliminaries, nor did he try to present a friendly image. "Why did you bring me here?"

"It is better here. We are bigger and stronger. We can protect you."

"What makes you think I need protection?"

"You would have frozen to death without the furs," the man gently reminded.

"Exactly who do you think I am?"

"You are a god. Like the other one."

"Like what other one?"

"Like the one who came before. They lost him. That is why we brought you here. We will protect you from being lost."

"Did you see the other one?"

"No. We heard about him."

"What did you hear?"

"He came from nowhere. He appeared before them. Then they lost him."

"Maybe he wanted to get lost."

"They were not able to protect him."

"What do you want of me? Why do you want me to stay here?"

"You are a god. You will bring us good fortune."

"What makes you think so? If you keep me here against my will and I get angry, I may bring you bad fortune."

The man said nothing. He had dropped to his knees upon entering and he stared at the floor. Evidently he was willing to risk the bad luck.

Bill got to his feet and began restlessly pacing the confines of the hut. "How do you people live? Where do you get your food? I haven't seen any animals around here."

"There are elk and buffalo. We have plenty of food."

"What about the rest of it—the vegetables—the things you have to grow?"

"There are many roots."

"No green things?"

"Green things? The roots are white and brown."

Obviously the man had never seen a green growing thing. He did not know what Bill was talking about.

"How far from this place do you travel?"

This caused the man to raise his eyes proudly. "We go as far as a dozen marches."

Bill estimated. At perhaps thirty miles a day that would be over three hundred miles. "Is the climate better south of here?"

"The climate?"

"The weather. Is there less snow and cold south of here?"

"It is always cold. There is snow everywhere."

Bill took a different tack. "Why are you hostile to everybody? Why do you kill all the time?"

"If we did not kill, they would kill us."

"Do you ever declare a truce with your enemies?"

"I don't know what a truce is."

"A time when there is peace—when neither side kills."

"No. That wouldn't be possible."

"Why not?"

"Because as soon as they got a chance they would kill us."

"But what do you gain by always killing?"

"We survive."

Bill was getting nowhere. If he had any idea of starting a peace movement among these natives, it suffered a blow.

Angry, he turned on the man. "I'm tried of this," he snapped. "I'm getting out of here. I'm going to walk out that door and go on my way."

The man placed his forehead against the floor and talked to the ground under him. "You must stay here. We must not let you go. No other village has a god. You must stay with us."

As he stared at the man in supreme frustration, Bill remembered a story he had once read. It was about a deep-sea diver who through some process came to the surface near a South Sea island. Superstitious natives, sure that he was a god, brought him ashore and put him on a throne. But he was not allowed to get out of his diving suit and he died there; but the natives continued to worship his dead body and then his skeleton.

This situation wasn't quite as bad as that, but he certainly wasn't in the happiest of situations.

He waved his hand angrily. "Go away. I want to sleep."

The old man got obediently to his feet and left as quietly as he'd come.

Bill threw himself on his furs and waited for the sound of the ceremonial dirge as he'd heard it in the other village. But it did not come. Evidently customs differed from village to village.

Finally his eyes closed and he went into a half doze.

This was broken as the door opened. Two furred figures entered, one behind the other.

"Who are you? What do you want?"

The lead figure stood silent, but the one behind him whispered a warning. "Not too loud. Be very quiet. Make too much noise and I'll be killed."

Bill came to his feet. He'd done nothing with the light and he could see how things were. The man behind had a knife poised at the neck of the man in front. The man in front was being very careful for fear the knife would be plunged into him.

"Gallow!" Bill exclaimed. "How did you get here?"

Flight into Sunlight

"HOW DID YOU FIND ME?" BILL whispered in amazement.

"I got back with your box. I hid it in some rocks near the village and saw them come and take you away. I got the box and followed."

The contrast revealed here stunned Bill. In a world where hostility and slaughter were the watchwords, Gallow had performed a heroic and seemingly impossible task. On a crutch and a broken leg he'd carried the scanner for miles. Then, having reached his goal, he'd picked it up and carried it for many more miles. The fact that the man seemed made of iron was only a minor wonder. More important, he was risking his life in a land where such risk was the height of idiocy.

"How did you get in here?"

"It wasn't too hard. The crutch doesn't mean anything because a lot of them are wounded and pulling themselves around. I got these black furs from one of the men they killed at the other village."

Black was the mark of the middle country people. Supplanting Gallow's lighter ones, they made him indistinguishable from the others.

"Who is this man?"

"I don't know. He probably came to see if you have enough wood for your fire. I came along with him."

"Do you think we can get away?"

"Put on your furs. We'll try."

Gallow stood with his knife at the man's throat while Bill dressed himself. Then instinct, or perhaps a slight movement, told Bill what Gallow contemplated. Bill sprang forward.

"No! You don't have to kill him."

"Only two can leave."

"All right. But killing isn't necessary. Here—"

There'd been a cloth over the food tray. Bill snatched it and jammed it into the man's mouth.

"A gag. That will keep him quiet. We'll tie him up with the leather thongs on his fur suit. We don't have to murder the man."

Gallow went along, but his manner indicated that he didn't think sparing the man made much sense. The task completed, Bill said "All right, we're going to try and escape, but where to? Where are we going after we get out—if we do?"

"I put your box in a rockpile out there."

"Why did you bring it with you?"

"I thought you might want it. It's what you disappear with, isn't it?"

"Yes, but how about you? If I can get to the box and it's working, I'll be all right. But that would leave you standing alone on the prairie."

"When you get to your box I'll go back to the other village."

"Won't they kill you?"

"You told them not to."

"But I won't be there to protect you."

"They'll do what you told them. They'll let me stay there until my leg is all right and then they'll give me salt."

"All right. If you say so. Let's find out if we're going anywhere."

They opened the door, went outside, and closed it after themselves. Bending forward and hiding their faces in their parkas, they turned left and sought to avoid the scattered guards.

Bill realized his main danger was his height. Walking erect, he stood out above Gallow. But, swathed in the furs, he was able to bend over. Also, he contrived to be helping the cripple he was with and thus stayed close to him.

The guards looked in their direction but, having seen them enter, their exit did not appear to be out of order.

"Go slow," Gallow whispered. "Don't start running or anything like that."

It seemed suddenly weird to Bill—Gallow giving these orders to one he considered a god. He would have liked to question Gallow as to what his exact feeling was, but this was hardly the time or the place. Also, he doubted if he'd learn much. Getting into the minds of these people was like trying to open a can of beans with a wet blotter.

But Gallow's caution was probably wise because Bill had never moved with such maddening slowness. They passed groups and pairs of the villagers at the snail's pace Gallow's crutch made logical. They seemed to make no progress at all and, if he hadn't been warned, Bill would probably have found himself traveling at least at a brisk walk without realizing it.

After what seemed hours they reached the far end of the village where it was relatively deserted and moved off across the open prairie. Now Bill blessed the snow and the sleet that he had previously cursed; blessed it because it thickened the air and formed a curtain of safety.

When they had reached a safe distance Gallow said, "Now we can go."

He suited the words by pushing the crutch out in

front of him and taking a long leap forward. Bill hurried to catch up. The crutch went forward again and Bill found that he had to break into a dogtrot to keep up with the indomitable native.

A short while later Gallow veered sharply to the right and stopped beside a pile of rocks. "I hid it in there."

Bill attacked the pile and soon he was able to reach in and haul the scanner out. It appeared to be undamaged and he could only hope its inner parts were not susceptible to sub-zero temperatures. The switch and the rheostat on the suit were warm and functionable under his fur suit.

Gallow stood balanced on his crutch. He had gone as far as his knowledge would permit. "What do you do now?"

"I have to find out—"

Gallow's hand on his arm stopped him. The native's eyes were narrowed as he bent his head into a listening position. "They're coming. The man got loose. We should have killed him."

It was too late to debate that point. "Get going," Bill said. He was unwinding the connection cord and pushing the loose end in through his fur suit.

"Get going! They'll kill you if they find you. I'll be all right. If they catch, me, they'll just take me back."

"I want to see," Gallow said stubbornly. "I want to tell my children I saw the god leave."

"Stay here and you won't have any children!" Bill cried.

"I'll stay."

The man was an idiot, Bill told himself wildly, but as he pulled the back of his inner suit around and inserted the plug, he had to admit Gallow was a very brave idiot.

His hands found the switch and the rheostat. He activated them.

And it was his last thought in this cheerless world that he would never know whether Gallow made it or not.

But it was his first thought in the next world that Gallow surely had. With the man's courage and strength and his iron will to survive, he would return to his own north country and tell his children and grandchildren about the days he spent with a god.

Then Bill was aware of soft grass beneath his feet and the warm yellow sun sending its glorious rays down from above.

The Law of All the Worlds

BILL'S ARRIVAL AT HIS NEXT DESTINATION WAS the strangest and most exciting experience of his life. But the excitement came from within himself, not from the delightful place at which he had arrived. During the transition, a thought formed clearly and sharply in his mind—words from his father's farewell letter: . . . *you are close to being a man, Bill—closer than you realize.* . . . He did not dwell upon this recollection, however. He only noted it in conjunction with the new feeling of poise and confidence with which he faced this new world; in connection with these and the firm, quiet conviction that he had come to the end of his pilgrimage; that he would find his father in this most beautiful of worlds.

He was in a park. There was flowers and trees and bushes. The air was as soft and caressing as a gentle hand. But this too, as he shucked off his outer garment of thick furs, he noted only in passing. There was something greater and far more important; something sensed rather than seen.

A feeling of at last coming home.

But the impression had to be challenged and questioned, because this was not home. He had not returned to the same plane from which he had started. Yet the sense of affinity persisted. Comfortable again, in slacks, a shirt, and pull-over sweater, Bill sat down on a bench to sort things out. And he realized that this very act was a proof of growing up. The old Bill would have rushed off in a feverish hunt for his father. The new one realized there was plenty of time and sought to do things in an orderly fashion, but with no doubt whatever in his mind that they would be done.

Almost musingly, he surveyed the setting into which he had been delivered. He had arrived early, the sun still low in the sky, which accounted for the solitude he'd found in the park. But this was obviously a huge urban area, a vast city. It was not greatly different from the one in which he had left Neal Adams, yet a difference did exist. It was difficult to define, but this one, even with its tall buildings, its beautiful parks, and its clean streets stretching away, was still not as scientifically advanced as the other. This seemed a contradiction. Had he gone backward? Bill was sure he had not. The principle of non-return had been pretty well established. Therefore, the explanation lay elsewhere, and Bill, who had asked so many questions of others, now found himself striving for his own answers.

He realized that the whole truth would never be known. The master-knot would remain eternally tied because each newly discovered answer posed a larger question. But Bill, on the basis of the multiple-plane theory, found it not difficult to visualize many solid worlds, many solid planes of existence, each extending out into what appeared to be an evolutionary maze, but which was certainly not a maze at all. His journey had proven to him that these evolutionary threads were no way correlated in time.

Then, quite suddenly, he *knew;* he knew why this world seemed like home; why he had such a sense of familiarity. This *was* the same world in the sense that it and the one he had left were parts of the same evolutionary pattern. Excited by this sudden conviction, Bill tried to reduce it to more understandable terms. He had gone out into the maze, had touched other threads alien to his own, but had come finally back to his own plane; back to the world native to his own existence. But how far beyond the time he had known? How many ages had passed? Or was that the way it worked?

Suddenly, Bill didn't care. His father was somewhere in this city, and when they met, it would be the first reunion of its kind ever to take place!

Then, just as suddenly, doubts assailed Bill. Both he and Neal had believed that the geographical travel patterns remained constant; that the scanner would direct them to the same locations his father had reached. The fact that he had gone through the world in which Neal had remained, tended to prove this. But the proof was not absolute. That could have been sheer coincidence.

Bill felt a touch of fright. What did a man fall back on when confusion set it? What was there when a man was forced to doubt? The answer came.

Faith. When trouble hits, there has to be faith.

Faith. Sitting there on the bench, staring at the skyline beyond, Bill took command of his mind and stilled his doubts. His father was there; somewhere close by. This was what he had been looking for. He'd found it and he would stay here. So all that remained was to find him and that shouldn't be too difficult. There were many ways to go about searching.

But none of them were necessary because, at that moment a voice from behind the bench sent goose pimples up Bill's spine. A quiet voice.

"Hello, son."

Bill came to his feet and turned. "Hello, Dad," he said quietly.

"You've changed, Bill."

His father's words made Bill realize all the more forcibly, that which he had sensed in himself. And the reunion was further proof. Bill had visualized it over the hours and the days; the joy, the elation. And these things were definitely a part of it. But it was not a highly emotional meeting of a father and an excited son. It was the reuniting of two men.

"We'll arrange to move your equipment," Sam Franklin said. "In the meantime, it will be perfectly safe here. How about some breakfast now. You must be hungry." Home was a small, neat cottage not unlike those of the faculty back at the University. "I've found a place for myself," Franklin said. "This is the Wayfield Clinic. Yet it's different from any clinic you have ever seen. Physical disease is practically unknown here, but the study and improvement of the human mind is really just beginning. There is much here that will surprise you."

Later, in response to Bill's questions, Sam Franklin said, "I couldn't tell you much in that letter, but I made my journey through the planes for two reasons. First because they were there and the journey was possible. And second, because I felt that my ability to do it obligated me." Franklin paused as he groped for words. "I think it has been the same with other men. Columbus, for instance. I think Columbus' belief in himself and his ability to go forward constituted an obligation he sensed."

Bill nodded. "But there is so much more—so many things I must find out."

His father laughed. "I'm afraid I'll disappoint you on that score. I'm no more of a scientific oracle than when I started out across the planes. I learned a few things, but even greater questions have presented themselves."

"We'll never know all of it, of course," Bill replied, "or even begin to, but there is one thing I wondered about. When I found myself in that park, I knew I was going to find you here. And there was a sense of— well, coming home, that I don't understand. This isn't home. This is not the world we left."

Franklin nodded in agreement. "I think we always seek answers that are too simple, Bill. I had that same feeling, that this is home—and I think we're partly right. There is much we will never learn, but I think this is a world of the same evolutionary progression. There is one unique factor that is common to both worlds. To put that factor in a word—it is *people*."

"I don't think I quite understand."

"In our other world there were many struggles, many mistakes, many wanderings along blind paths, but always with a single goal in mind—the freeing and the elevation of the human spirit. After every fall, our world became rededicated to that principle—the upward struggle of the human spirit. On other planes, even more advanced than ours, this was forgotten in preoccupation with scientific advancement, easier ways of life, a belief that comfort, ease, and pleasure were the right goals of mankind. Our world went through such stages, but each time it returned to basic struggle."

Bill's face brightened with excitement. "That was

it! That must have been what I found lacking in the beautiful world where I left Neal. It was all ease, all comfort. They believed they had found the answer. But something was missing."

Franklin smiled and there was pride in his look; pride in the instinctive perception he found in Bill. "You're right, son. They believed that the ultimate of human destiny is to master the machine and make it their servant."

Bill's eyes turned vague. "Do you think they are right?"

"What's your opinion."

"I think they are wrong."

"I felt the same way. That was why I left their plane —why I found this one, where the infinite possibilities of the human development toward individual perfection is the ultimate aim."

"Then, in a sense, we *have* come home, haven't we Dad?"

"Yes, son," Sam Franklin said quietly. "Back to the wonderful, exciting world we left."

Lester Del Rey is no stranger to readers of
science fiction and science fact. Several of his books
have received special notice; *Marooned on Mars* received a Boys' Club of American Award, and *Rockets
through Space* won the Thomas Alva Edison Award
for the best science book in the children's book field
in 1960. It was praised by scientists as demonstrating
a keen understanding of the problems involved in
space travel.

A long series of occupations preceded Mr. Del Rey's
highly successful writing career. After graduating from
George Washington University in Washington, D.C.,
he worked at various times as a carpenter, hotel clerk,
farmer, photographer, and advertising man. His in-
terests cover as wide a range as his occupations have—
from philology, linguistics, and history to cooking,
cabinetmaking, and the repairing of old typewriters,
which he buys for that express purpose.